About the Author

Julie is a former medical practice administrator and *Long Shadows* is her first full length novel. She has three children and lives in West Sussex with her husband Clive. They regularly walk in the Lake District and it was perhaps inevitable that this setting became the backdrop for the novel.

Dedication

I would like to dedicate this work to Will who encouraged and cajoled me to write my novel and critiqued every chapter as it rolled off my laptop into his inbox. He also provided inspiration for one of the crimes, for which I am very grateful.

Julie Haiselden

LONG SHADOWS

Copyright © Julie Haiselden

The right of Julie Haiselden to be identified as author of this work has been asserted by her in accordance with section 77 and 78 of the Copyright, Designs and Patents Act 1988.

All rights reserved. No part of this publication may be reproduced, stored in a retrieval system, or transmitted in any form or by any means, electronic, mechanical, photocopying, recording, or otherwise, without the prior permission of the publishers.

Any person who commits any unauthorized act in relation to this publication may be liable to criminal prosecution and civil claims for damages.

A CIP catalogue record for this title is available from the British Library.

ISBN 978 1 84963 988 0

www.austinmacauley.com

First Published (2015)
Austin Macauley Publishers Ltd.
25 Canada Square
Canary Wharf
London
E14 5LB

Printed and bound in Great Britain

Acknowledgments

Thank you to Clive who has had to suffer my insecurities and tantrums over the past few months as my characters took over my life. Unbelievably he still wants to live with me – although he has said he is open to offers while I am writing the next book.

Chapter 1

A New Beginning – 1988/9

Lizzie Tennyson sat at her dressing table and looked at herself in the mirror as she remembered the first time she had seen the Blenthorne Inn. She picked up her brush and began to pull it through her damp shoulder length light brown hair as she switched on her hairdryer. The gentle purr of the dryer and the comforting warmth being emitted gave her time to ponder the events that had led her here.

It had been a cold and thoroughly miserable September morning. They left the relative comfort of their B&B in the pleasant market town of Keswick in central Cumbria and drove for about half an hour to the picturesque village of Blenthorne.

Lizzie had read up about Blenthorne when her husband Richard had first mentioned the place – it had a newsagents, general store and post office, a church and village hall, a tourist information centre with public toilets attached – not open all year round – a couple of outdoor clothing retailers, a tea shop, a hotel and of course the obligatory tat shop for visitors to buy presents for friends and relatives as unwanted keepsakes of their holiday.

It had a population of about five hundred people, which increased during the warmer months when tourists came to walk the fells or were in the area to attempt to walk from St Bees in the west to Robin Hood's Bay in the east. That was becoming the thing to do – with an increasing number of tourists from Europe and The United States.

About a quarter of a mile from the heart of the village was the Blenthorne Inn, or "the pub" as Lizzie had taken to thinking of it.

She could not imagine what had actually taken possession of Richard in his quest for a new life. Things had been going smoothly, well quite smoothly, he worked in the City for an investment bank and she worked part time as a nurse at the local hospital. She liked her life and enjoyed the company of other young mums who lived in the small market town where she had grown up in the south east of England, the only child of a garage mechanic and sub-postmistress.

She had had a relatively happy childhood, only marred by the death of her best friend Caroline in a swimming accident whilst on holiday in Cornwall. That had been terrible, the worst event in her young life. Starting the new term at school the following September with Caroline's peg empty in the cloakroom and her vacant desk a sad reminder of what Lizzie had lost. She often thought she could hear Caroline laughing in the playground, only to turn round to find it was someone else entirely. It had taken Lizzie a long time to come to terms with the loss of her friend and many a night she cried into her pillow so that her parents would not hear. Slowly, as she grew older, the memory of Caroline faded but never completely left her.

After school and college she had qualified as a nurse, married and after she had given birth to Alex, her much longed for child, her life took on a happy and familiar pattern. She enjoyed child-centred activities, coffee mornings, weekly visits to the gym and the odd evening out with her girlfriends.

She and Richard were reasonably affluent and holidayed abroad once each year to the usual tourist destinations of Spain and Greece, along with an annual trip to the Lake District where they stayed in various locations. They owned their own house, well at least a part of it. The bank owned the rest but the mortgage was not crippling and it appeared the value of the property had doubled in the time they had lived in it.

They had hit a sticky patch when Richard confessed to an affair after several years of what Lizzie believed to be a successful marriage. Her world was temporarily turned upside down. She always believed that if such a thing should happen she would have no hesitation in ending the relationship. However when it actually did, she realised that grand declarations were fine in theory but the harsh reality was that her circumstances would be significantly reduced if she did leave Richard. They had known each other on and off since childhood and had got together after she finished her nursing diploma. She really didn't know if she was brave enough to survive alone.

He had begged her to stay. He did not know what had come over him, he had been flattered by the attention, excited by the deception, but she had to believe him when he said he was shattered to have jeopardised their life together as a family and he would do anything, absolutely anything if she would forgive him.

After a lot of tears, shouting, soul-searching and recriminations, they had finally worked through it and things had returned to something like normal and Lizzie had just started to believe they could still have a future together.

Richard felt what they needed was a fresh start. He said he did not want to think of their lives stretching before them in the same predictable routine. He wanted something more, a challenge, a new life away from the grind of the daily commute and the shackles of the wheeler dealer world in which he lived during the week. He did not want them to grow old feeling that they had missed out.

He had come up with several business ideas, including a sheep farm in Wales and going to live in Australia, where apparently there was a shortage of nurses. His plan was for Lizzie to work while he searched for a niche for himself and in the short term, he would be a house husband and look after Alex.

With the introduction of each new idea, Lizzie had questioned him regarding the practicalities, such as, what did he know about sheep or indeed farming for that matter? What was the attraction for Australia? Did he know anyone who lived there? What was the cost of living like? Would he not miss his friends and his life in England? Did he realise the implications of being a house husband and full-time homemaker? She thought not.

Usually this was enough food for thought to keep him occupied for a few weeks until he forgot about it or an even better proposition superseded it. However then he had hit upon the Lake District idea. Why not buy a business where they could live and work together; bring up their son in a healthy environment surrounded by countryside and fresh air. They loved the Lake District so where better? No matter how much Lizzie played devil's advocate, Richard always countered her objections with solutions that he was clearly making up on the hoof.

He stumbled on the idea of a pub rather by chance. He had gone for a drink with a mate one evening to their local and upon arrival, it was clear the landlord was struggling. His regular barman was on holiday and the agency replacement had let him down. Whilst Richard had never in his life pulled a pint, he offered his help, such as it was. He came home elated. After grappling with the intricacies of the till and a few spillages, he had apparently been an invaluable asset to the smooth running of the establishment, so much so that the landlord had asked if he would be free to help out until his regular barman returned!

After that, he was at the pub whenever he had some spare time to learn as much as he could about running the business. He was naturally gregarious and could turn on the charm when needed so chatting with "the punters", as he had taken to calling the customers, came easily to him. The more his confidence grew, the more he felt certain this was the life they were destined for. He studied for his personal publican's licence and passed without a problem. This only served to reinforce his conviction that without any doubt this was the way forward. This heralded their new beginning!

After liaising with local estate agents and several trips to view available properties in various parts of the area without her and Alex, Richard had finally came home after one such visit, to excitedly announce he had found the ideal place for them.

Until then Lizzie had thought maybe the whole thing might go the way of his other ideas and as much as she loved visiting the Lakes for a week or two each year, she did not actually want to live there. But now that he had found somewhere, she realised she could sink her head in the sand no longer. If she wanted their marriage to work, she had to indulge him by going to see the place, feigning interest and when she had considered the proposal thoroughly – talk him out of it.

Lizzie smiled to herself as she continued to dry her hair with her reflection looking back at her. She could hear the sound of voices wafting up from downstairs. They could manage for now. The soporific sound of the dryer allowed her to continue to reminisce.

Her first sight of the pub came as they drove through a misty murky Blenthorne and there it was standing in front of them, looming out of its damp and dreary surroundings like a macabre monster rearing its head from a lonely lagoon.

As they climbed out of the car Lizzie felt her hair being flattened to the sides of her face by the chilly wind as small speckles of drizzle settled on her nose and cheeks. She shivered as she glanced at Richard who had a look of excited expectation on his face. He had leapt out of the car and almost ran to meet the estate agent for their planned inspection of the property.

Lizzie shut her door and turned to the door behind her as they still used the child locks when Alex was on board – he climbed out, clearly glad to be free from the confines of the car.

'Stay with me please Alex,' Lizzie called as her son took off at pace towards a very dilapidated looking swing in an overgrown area of lawn.

She looked around and shuddered as she saw the cold drab building before her with the silent unwelcoming fells looking down menacingly in the background. Her feet crunched loudly on the stones beneath. She felt ever so slightly sick. Was this really happening?

She had a sense of complete isolation and wretchedness, miles from the nearest town without a friendly face in sight. To be fair, the estate agent was smiling encouragingly in his expensive looking dark suit and very loud tie but of course he wanted to sell them the lease on the place so his demeanour was hardly what Lizzie would call sincere. Richard introduced them but she felt so dejected that the agent's name didn't even register in Lizzie's brain.

The pub lived up, or rather down, to her expectations completely. Every conceivable frightful feature was waiting for her, just as she had feared it would be. As they walked through the door the atmosphere felt dank, musty and oppressive. There was dust over most surfaces and the odd cobweb with resident spider. The rooms were dark and unattractive. Their feet seemed to echo on the floors as did their voices in the stale air. However where she saw a problem, Richard saw potential. Lizzie wanted to cry.

It was quite a large property, built, the agent had been reliably informed, in about 1780 and it had originally been used as a coaching inn. It comprised two bar areas with one set up with a few tables for dining. The other was an archetypal old fashioned public bar with a low ceiling, fireplace, beams and brass. Lizzie found herself looking round for a spittoon but thankfully, she couldn't see one. Her nose wrinkled in disgust when she realised she had inadvertently placed her hand on the bar and some sort of gloopy mess had engulfed it. Alex was being rather petulant.

'Mum, I don't like it here, please can we go now?' If only they could she thought unhappily as she searched through her handbag for a tissue.

She smiled down at Alex with as much sincerity as she could muster.

'Soon darling, soon,' she replied.

Although all things are relative when one is in a mood of melancholia and despondency, Lizzie had to concede that the kitchen was a pleasant surprise.

It did seem that the previous owners had refitted it, so it would be possible to provide meals in a reasonable quantity. This was always assuming of course that they could afford some staff in the fullness of time. The cooker was of the large industrial range type with a substantial hot plate and there were stainless steel drawers and cupboards under work surfaces along each wall, with a central island also constructed of stainless steel. There was a free standing fridge freezer and a walk-in larder, along with two sinks set apart to allow one area for food preparation and one for washing up. Appropriate implements and utensils appeared to be in place, all covered in a layer of dust and in need of a good clean, Lizzie thought.

Leading off from the kitchen was a utility room which housed a butler sink and wooden draining board, a large dishwasher and washing machine with work surfaces and cupboards above, along with a huge chest freezer – at least there was sufficient storage for multiple purchasing; necessary for the type of weather they could expect in winter when the roads might well be impassable thought Lizzie being practical. The back door was to the left of the sink.

Lizzie noticed that some of the red quarry tiles were broken on the floor of the utility room and a bit of carpet had been strategically placed over these, presumably not only to try to hide them but to stop anyone from actually tripping over.

Going back through the kitchen, another door from the hall revealed a reasonable sized office with a wooden desk and chair behind and a couple of upright chairs facing it. The décor here was also dark, dreary and dated and there was a smell of stale smoke pervading the room. Lizzie looked towards the grubby ashtray with repugnance. Two sets of public toilets made up the ground floor; Lizzie decided to spare herself an inspection of these. There was also a door leading to the cellar. Again Lizzie passed. Richard had a cursory inspection and professed himself satisfied with what he had seen below.

Upstairs revealed two equally tired looking guest rooms with en-suite facilities that were fitted out in avocado green. Nice. These the agent gushed, were just waiting to be rented out! The weekly income generated would add substantially to their profits. Lizzie easily managed to resist any urge to cheer at this wonderful prospect.

Richard though was lapping it up. He was looking at the agent and nodding enthusiastically with a big grin on his face, his mouth slightly open. The agent said he had saved their quarters to last as he unlocked the private apartment with a flourish. Richard bounded in through the door like an excitable puppy. Lizzie's entrance was less dramatic.

In the private apartment there were two bedrooms, both in need of redecorating and currently adorned with ghastly pink flowery wallpaper, a lot of which was peeling from the walls – probably damp thought Lizzie grimly.

There was also a bathroom – pale blue this time rather than avocado Lizzie was pleased to note, however, the bath had a hand-held shower over it with a slightly perished rubber hose which divided into two to cover the hot and cold taps. This was set off with the addition of a shower curtain draped inside the bath. She wondered what colour it had been originally, it appeared now to be a sort of grey with a fetching edge of mould at the bottom and small black spots dotted throughout. She managed to reproduce a very good impersonation of her mother as she wrinkled her nose and ran her fingers over the window sill. As she thought, mildew – and yes, her eyes were not deceiving her – there was a manky looking toothbrush lying in the wash basin with what appeared to be advanced alopecia. It could not get worse – could it?

The eagle eyed estate agent was obviously aware of her "lack of positive feel for the place" as he put it. He explained rapidly that the previous tenants had formulated many plans for improvements which would make all the difference in the world and he could tell she was a woman of foresight, discernment and imagination who could see beyond the current décor ... He talked on as Lizzie tuned out.

They left the bathroom and made their way into a smallish kitchen area which had seen better days. Blue laminate worktops, red linoleum on the floor and a flowery orange blind at the window – well at least the bad taste was consistent.

Lizzie noted the range of cupboards detailed in the agents' particulars. To be fair, they did not say the cupboards were matching, so really she should not be surprised that they looked like they had been bought at a jumble sale and screwed to the walls at varying heights and angles by someone in a state of inebriation. She tried tipping her head, but no, they still didn't look straight. Two had been painted a pale blue colour and the rest were pine. Richard saw none of this. He just saw their dream home with a business attached that was going to make them both happy and rich. Lizzie still wanted to cry.

In the lounge area the wallpaper was circa mid-70s with a black background and huge orange flowers. The carpet was light blue and threadbare. There was pine cladding on the fireplace chimney. An orange nodding dog sat forlornly on one of the window sills in front of a slightly torn grubby looking net curtain. Lizzie wiped a tear from her eye and hoped no one noticed.

They made their way downstairs and left the building for the outside space.

This was set to the side of the pub and overgrown with weeds and brambles. There was a play area of sorts with a slide pitifully peeping out from the undergrowth entangled with bindweed. The swing that Alex had been heading for earlier stood next to it, looking equally forlorn. There was a patio to the back of the building – ideal for those hot summer days the agent enthused. Lizzie wondered how well he actually knew the area, as from some of her previous visits she could barely remember a hot summer day!

The other side comprised a large barn which, according to the agent, was originally used to stable teams of horses for stage and mail coaches. In addition there was another small outbuilding standing just to the left of the barn. With planning permission which would almost certainly be granted, they could renovate the barn and divide it into two or three self-contained holiday rentals. They would still have outside storage space afforded by the smaller outbuilding; the agent smiled and paused for breath.

Richard's eyes shone out from the gloom of the day.

'Or the barn could be turned into a restaurant!' he said, unable to keep the elation out of his voice.

'Indeed,' said the agent encouragingly, not that Richard needed any more encouragement. 'A restaurant would be a splendid idea – I would certainly dine here!'

Lizzie winced at the mutual love-in that seemed to be developing between Richard and the agent and asked why the previous tenants had left. Clearly anticipating the question, the agent launched into a spiel about a death in the family which had meant they could not stay in the area much as they loved it and were making a success of the place.

Richard hushed her up quickly by saying he was quite happy with the figures he had seen at his first inspection and knew there was money to be made here. So firmly put in her place, Lizzie lapsed into silence. She subsequently found out that the wife of the previous landlord had hated living there so much that she had given her husband an ultimatum - they left together or she left alone.

As they finished their inspection Richard was pumping the agent's hand with gusto, Lizzie was hoping desperately that he was not actually going to hug him. She marched purposefully to the car and made sure Alex had strapped himself into his seat, fighting back her tears as she did so.

They had travelled home more or less in silence, stopping off on the way at a couple of motorway service stations for food and loo breaks. During the journey the only sound, other than the rhythmical whir of the engine, was the car radio with every song seeming to be a lament about a broken heart. How apt Lizzie thought. Her heart felt so heavy, she wasn't at all sure it was still situated in her chest cavity.

Once home they discussed the matter thoroughly from all angles, as Richard liked to put it. Lizzie's interpretation to friends was that they argued day and night for a week.

In the end she had given in, as she always knew she would. Richard had taken his business plan to the bank and had his idea approved.

When they told her parents the news, her mother had folded her arms under her ample chest, sniffed loudly and whispered to Lizzie that she and Alex could come and live with them any time they wanted. Lizzie shivered involuntarily.

They had been given a wonderful send off by their friends and neighbours with drinks parties and invites to dinner, culminating in a huge gathering at a local hall with music and food all arranged behind Lizzie's back – she smiled and made the right noises but actually she hated surprises.

She tried to put a brave face on things and everyone made encouraging noises – all secretly glad it was her and not them that were being whisked away to start a new life at the back of beyond with all the insecurity and uncertainty this would bring.

Richard had taken voluntary redundancy from the City and she had left her nursing job. They had sunk the equity from the sale of their house, their savings and the redundancy money into this project and now they had to make it work. Ten months later they had taken up residence.

At the age of thirty-two Lizzie Tennyson was entering the next chapter of her life. She hoped it was a positive one.

*

When they arrived they got down to work straightaway. They scrubbed and polished and vacuumed until the place at least looked presentable. Richard had given Lizzie a crash course on measuring out drinks as well as working the till.

Three days after they moved in Alex started at nearby Rowendale Primary School. He had coped well with the move and leaving his friends but was clearly anxious about what lay ahead, particularly when he put on his new school uniform for his first day. Lizzie felt very sorry for him as she brushed his hair and straightened his tie. They had arranged a meeting with his class teacher and the head-teacher the day before and so he knew what to expect to some extent but even so, he kept asking her questions she could not answer.

'Will I have anyone to sit with?'

'Will the other children be nice to me?'

'Do I take my book bag into the classroom and what about my PE kit?'

Lizzie reassured him as best she could and told him that she would be waiting for him at home time.

She had spent the first day with her stomach twisted into a knot, listening out for the phone, just in case the school rang. She imagined Alex all alone in a strange place knowing no-one and getting sadder by the minute. When she tried to talk to

Richard he told her to stop worrying; as usual, he had no ability to empathise with what she was feeling. She counted the minutes until she could respectably drive to the school to wait for the afternoon bell.

As it transpired, Alex had in fact had a far better day than Lizzie. He came rushing out the door saying that a boy called Owen had been assigned to look after him and everyone had wanted to talk to him at break-time. His teacher Mrs Howard had been very nice and he didn't think it would be too bad after all.

Thankfully he settled very quickly, demonstrating that in fact he was far more resilient than Lizzie gave him credit for.

The previous weekend was the first time they were open for business. They thought it would take a while for word to get around that the Blenthorne Inn, or "the Blenny" as the locals called it, was open again. Lizzie checked at least half a dozen times that everything was looking as she would wish it before they unlocked the door for their first evening's trading.

About ten minutes after opening time, a large middle-aged man with greying hair walked or rather shuffled into the public bar, wiping his nose on the back of his hand as he did so. Lizzie observed this process with slight revulsion but hoped it did not show on her face. Could not offend their first patron!

'You must be the new landlady,' he had said somewhat gratuitously.

'Indeed yes!' replied Lizzie hoping she sounded cheerful and welcoming. 'What can I get for you; do you live around here?' she asked as she gravitated towards the beer pumps – he didn't look like a vodka and tonic sort of chap.

'Well yes, yes I live nearby. I'll have a pint of bitter if you please – it's nice to see this old place open again. I'm a painter and decorator by trade you know but I used to work here, part time of course – for the previous landlord like – the name is Bert, Bert Bumstead'.

'How nice to meet you Bert,' said Lizzie attempting to keep her face straight as she shook his outstretched hand with a degree of trepidation, surreptitiously wiping her own hand down the right hand side of her jeans afterwards. 'What did you do here – bar work or ...?'

'That's right behind the bar mostly; I ran this bar and Bob and Rosie concentrated on the other one. I can change a barrel, clean the pipework, take deliveries, go to the wholesalers, anything you like really. Don't mind the pots and slops either – quite happy to do that for you.'

Lizzie thought this was turning into a job interview rather than a social encounter.

'Point is Mrs ... um Mrs ...'

'Tennyson, call me Lizzie,' helped Lizzie.

'Well the point is, if you are needing somebody and I think you might be as it's an awful lot of work for two people, particularly with a young child, well I would be happy to come back.'

'I know the locals you see, they like to come in of an evening for a quiet pint – nice for them to see a friendly face – not that you aren't friendly Lizzie, I'm sure you are.' Bert Bumstead spluttered into silence and looked at Lizzie hopefully, rather red in the face. Lizzie felt quite sorry for him; he was clearly hoping to get his job back.

He had certainly done his homework she thought. He knew they had Alex and were planning to try to manage things until they could get on their feet. She realised that every conversation she had had in the village shop had probably been broadcast for miles.

'You know Bert, I think we could do with someone, I would like to do a bit of cooking to serve in the other bar and hopefully get some rentals out of the rooms upstairs, so running this bar too, well, I think it would be rather a lot. I'll need to talk to my husband obviously but how about I take your phone number and ring you tomorrow?'

Bert sighed, obviously feeling a bit more optimistic.

'Ah, thank you Mrs ... Lizzie. As I said, I have my own painting and decorating business as well, so any help you need with sprucing up the place, odd jobs and the like, well you just let me know. Things are a bit tight at home and this would make so much difference to us, particularly with the wedding coming up; my daughter Maggie, she's getting married. She has done the odd shift too if you are interested? Well maybe not at the moment as you are only just getting settled.'

Lizzie served Bert his pint, on the house as a goodwill gesture. It subsequently appeared to her that he somehow seemed to have a sort of telepathic connection to every house in the village. She didn't see him leave to make a phone call but within half an hour the public bar was heaving. Bert introduced everyone to Lizzie as they came in – however by the fourth customer she had given up trying to remember their names. She called Richard through from the lounge bar to help serve but he had just had a group of six walkers arrive wanting to look at the supper menu.

So before she knew it she had forgotten she was supposed to ask Richard about taking Bert on.

'Hey Bert, stop gassing and get yourself behind this bar; how's a girl supposed to cope alone?' Lizzie demanded rhetorically with her hands on her hips.

Bert shot round to the other side of the bar at a speed that belied his size.

'You just leave this to me Mrs ... Lizzie. Prices the same? Good,' said Bert answering his own question. 'I can manage this lot. You go and see what the walkers in the lounge bar want to eat.'

'What? You think I can rustle up supper for six just like that?' stammered Lizzie. 'We are not doing food yet.'

'Come on girl, I'm here to help now – you must have got something in the fridge,' said Bert forgetting completely that he was on his best behaviour and speaking to her in the same way he would have spoken to his daughter.

Lizzie found herself being pushed into the kitchen by Bert and wondered just who was employing whom.

She recovered her composure and went through into the lounge bar to say they were not really equipped as yet to provide a full menu but if the customers would be happy with soup and ploughman's or omelettes and salad she could accommodate them with pleasure. They all nodded in agreement and ordered another round of drinks.

Within less than half an hour she had prepared six soups, followed by two omelettes with salad and four ploughman's platters. She had even cobbled together a fruit crumble with custard in case they wanted a sweet course. She casually mentioned this as she collected their empty plates and the diners all looked at each other and then nodded enthusiastically at her. Six portions of dessert were duly served without delay.

Richard of course took full credit for the success of their first evening's trading as he happily counted the takings.

By the time she went to bed, Lizzie felt her confidence soar – she had taken on their first member of staff and prepared dinner for six with a bit of initiative and improvisation – maybe they could make this work after all? Time would tell.

*

She switched off her hairdryer and put it down on the dressing table. All in all, not a bad baptism into the pub trade she decided. She put her hair up into a ponytail and put a final finish to her lipstick. The result wasn't too unpleasant – she would never win any beauty contests but she scrubbed up okay – even if she was what her mother liked to call "big boned". Her father had reassured her there was nothing wrong with being strong and "built-to-last".

She got up and walked over to the bedroom door ready to start another hectic day. Richard was calling her from downstairs. She thought ironically it would actually be nice if they had a day off to go and enjoy some of the area instead of working all the time – in fact this pub could be anywhere in the county for all she saw of the Lake District.

Oh well plenty of time for that she thought wistfully. Perhaps it was just as well she didn't know what was waiting for her in the years ahead.

Chapter 2

Richard – 1991/2

Richard Tennyson climbed into his dark blue family saloon car for the familiar journey to Carlisle. He responded to a wave from a farmer on a passing tractor. He knew the bloke by sight but no more. Lizzie would know all about him of course, she made sure she remembered everyone she came in contact with and she had also memorised their children's names so that she could enquire as to their progress in school and suchlike. He wasn't particularly interested in getting too friendly with the locals as they didn't really spend enough money at the inn to make it worth his while. However, he had to concede her approach seemed to be paying off as she was making quite an impact in the neighbourhood.

It was hard to believe that a year and a half had passed since the three of them had arrived in Blenthorne. Alex had settled well at school and in the early days Lizzie made sure she invited lots of his classmates round for tea to maximise his chances of acceptance.

Unfortunately it hadn't been quite the wonderful idyll that Richard had hoped. For a start, there was so little time to do anything other than work. The business was all consuming with the day-to-day running, ideas for the renovation of the inn itself and the future development of the site, as they had decided to incorporate a restaurant in what was currently the old barn – finance permitting.

For the first year they had needed to consolidate themselves and could not consider any expansion until they knew their income would sustain it. However, the figures were looking good which meant he could go ahead and find an architect. One had been recommended, so he needed to make contact to get some plans drawn up. Thereafter he needed to investigate the appropriate planning permissions and present his business plan to the bank. His brain started to whirl; there were really not enough hours in the day.

As he started the engine, Richard smiled quietly to himself remembering ironically it was he who had dragged Lizzie practically kicking and screaming into this dream of his but it was she that had thrown herself into the project heart and soul.

She loved the place, the people and the life; she had fitted in from the first day. She and Bert, the parochial old codger she insisted on employing, were now a well-known double act. Still it worked in his favour as it gave him time to look after the overall running of the place and pursue plans for the future.

Lizzie had enrolled onto a cookery course, graduating from all things mince to chicken and pork and expanding the menu accordingly. She had made friends, the locals loved her and she had embedded herself into the very heart of the community. How she found the time Richard would never know, she worked tirelessly and he could not fault her for that.

She had got the darts team going again and the Blenthorne Inn was certainly not disgracing itself in the local league. She was raising money for the church roof – what church didn't have a leaky roof thought Richard with a smile – and she had become involved in the flagging amateur dramatic society.

She was currently helping to plan a pantomime for the following Christmas – it did seem a bit premature as it was only February but Lizzie believed it was all in the preparation. Strike early to avoid people making excuses she had said. No one had seen the like of such a production in Blenthorne and the surrounding villages and hamlets for over ten years. He had to admit the venture was drawing the whole community together; with notices around the area and a banner in the public bar to announce that auditions would start in May. He had even seen one on the back of the tractor that had just driven past him as he set off. It seemed that most families had at least one member who was thinking of getting involved in the production. He was currently resisting all pressure to try for the part of an ugly sister or cousin or some such – of which there were going to be five apparently, as there was no shortage of suitable candidates!

He turned from their quiet village road onto the main route for Carlisle. Not too much traffic at this time of year he thought so he should make good time. During the summer months the roads were pretty congested, not that he was complaining, the business the visitors brought to the area was essential for the place as a whole. There was also a bit of an influx around Christmas but that had all died down now thankfully.

They had begun quietly at the inn, just seeing to start with if they could keep their heads above water. As time went by they realised they were obviously doing something right, as their small profit margin grew each time they did the accounts. The two guest rooms were now full more often than not, apart from in the depths of winter.

Several of their friends had been true to their word and had made the pilgrimage north to see Richard and Lizzie in their new home. Two couples had come back twice, so they realised it was not just loyalty that was attracting them, they must really enjoy what the area in general and the inn in particular were able to offer, which was encouraging. They had decorated the guest rooms in understated quiet shades of pale green, as Lizzie said that way the terrible avocado bathroom suites looked deliberate, as they certainly could not afford to replace them at the moment.

Lizzie was keen to get their quarters refurbished but that was low on the list of priorities as no one other than themselves saw the flat, well no one that mattered anyway, he knew that Lizzie invited her friends round sometimes. He had more important things to worry about.

Richard dropped into a low gear and stopped at the roundabout, turning on the windscreen wipers as the mist which seemed ever-present at this time of year had turned to drizzle, he also directed a bit of heat onto the windscreen to stop it from misting up.

Lizzie wanted to decorate the two bars, however Richard saw more business potential in amalgamating them, thereby increasing the capacity for dining and attracting larger parties. Lizzie worried about "her locals" as she referred to them. The

Blenny was at the heart of village life. He had made the point as strongly as possible that keeping the locals happy did not make good business sense. True, many people used the public bar, however they managed to make their drinks last for hours and Richard had calculated that on average each local punter bought a pint and a half an evening.

Against this was the profit that was being generated by the lounge bar with tourists and walkers coming in and spending money freely. Most arrived and had a round of drinks and a rest and of course the obligatory trip to the toilet after walking for hours. He made a point of drawing attention to their lunch and supper menu in his pseudo-bonhomie style. Hardly anyone left without buying at least a sandwich, which would obviously necessitate another round of drinks to wash it down. He also noticed that people who were self-catering patronised the inn several times during their stay, so that was also encouraging.

Lizzie had rejected the amalgamation idea of course; she could not see that this was the way forward, at least until they got the restaurant up and running. She was encouraging the hangers-on not only with darts, but she had installed some sort of medieval coin board game oddity and a type of billiard pinball table amusement – goodness knows where she had got them from; he could not believe his eyes when they were delivered. It was all so old fashioned and dated, not what he wanted at all. More to the point, the new additions were taking up valuable table space where more punters could be accommodated.

He was thinking of contacting some coach holiday companies to see if they would be interested in stopping off during the quiet season for their passengers to have a drink, a round of sandwiches and a comfort break – there was a bit in the village to keep them amused for an hour or two before going on to the next place – would go down well with foreign tourists he thought – he would look into that, time permitting.

He slowed down as he came up behind a cyclist. There was a bend ahead and he could not see if it was safe to overtake – oh well, gear change, foot down, he would do it anyway – the cyclist would have to swerve into the verge if they met an oncoming vehicle. No problem. The road was clear in front of him.

There was also the problem of walkers coming in off the fells and using the facilities without buying any refreshments. The geography of the place meant they could have direct access to the toilets without going through either of the bars. Richard felt this was not on.

Lizzie hated the idea, but he planned to install keypad locks on the outer toilet doors so that people would have to get the combination from one or other of the bars before gaining access to the toilets. If they didn't want to buy a drink they could pay for the conveniences or use the public ones when they were open. When it was off season and the public amenities were shut, the walkers could go elsewhere, he was not a charity. People could only expect to use what they paid for. Lizzie maintained that if they barred people from using the facilities, they would just pee – or worse – in her petunias. She could be very provincial sometimes.

She was an amazing woman in many ways but just too soft, she had no business brain. However, she would come round, she always did. He was confident that within a few weeks not only would they have locks on the toilets; they would be well on the way to knocking the two bars into one – he must get some quotes organised soon. When the time came to sell the place, it would be generating a healthy turnover with a good profit margin if he had anything to do with it. Yes, things would work out in the end – it was just a matter of getting the planning right.

He was on the outskirts of Carlisle by this time. As he neared his destination he thought the brakes felt a bit spongy, he would drop by the garage sometime in the next few days to get them looked at.

*

Later that day Lizzie was just tucking Alex up in bed and wondering what time Richard would be home. She knew he had gone into Carlisle earlier to look at some samples for the flooring downstairs. She favoured a stone floor in the public bar; he was still clinging to the idea of knocking the two bars into one. Whilst she usually gave in and let him have his way, this time she was standing firm. Her locals would not be pushed out.

Alex wanted to talk to her about school after he climbed into bed. It was their quiet time and one which she or Richard preserved every night. They were so caught up each day with running the pub, they needed to have some ring-fenced time with their child – otherwise what on earth were they doing it all for? The idea was a better life and it could not be better if they never had any quality time with Alex. They chatted happily and he assured her that he had no homework she didn't know about and he was excited about being chosen for the rugby team for the next inter-house match.

She was very pleased that Alex had settled so readily, he was enjoying school and seemed popular; it appeared that hardly a week went by without another party invitation being enthusiastically pulled out of his school bag when he got home.

'I can go Mum, can't I?' he would say, his eyes wide and pleading.

'When have I ever said no,' said Lizzie indulgently as she smiled at him thinking that would be another present to remember to buy.

She was very lucky, there were a few other young mums around the village with children at the school and they often took it in turns to run the children to and fro, so that made life easier for them all. She would sometimes have a few friends round while Bert was setting up in the morning before opening, or for a cup of tea in the afternoon.

'Of course I can manage! I'll let you know when I am in my dotage,' muttered Bert. He encouraged her to spend some time socialising. 'Good for business. The girls will go home and tell their husbands how welcome you made them and they will all come back for a drink and a meal hopefully!' he said wiping his nose on the back of his hand.

'Why Bert, you are beginning to sound just like Richard!' laughed Lizzie.

Bert mumbled something inaudible under his breath as he shuffled towards the cellar door.

Her new friends all laughed at her wonky cupboards in the upstairs flat, but readily enjoyed her hospitality and for her part she loved being accepted by her neighbours, many of whom had been born nearby.

She got up from Alex's bed, said goodnight and God bless as she drew his curtains together at the window. His room looked out over the back of the building. She saw the rain coming down in stair rods as she wiped away the condensation from the inside of the window and peered casually down into the car park. She was just about to turn away when she noticed a police car drawing up into an available parking space. She was not too concerned; they ran a tight ship and never flouted any licencing laws.

As she went downstairs, she heard a knock at the back door. When she opened it, she saw Gary Carmichael, a tall slim dark haired young PC whom she knew by sight.

'My goodness officer, what brings you here on such a filthy night – come in out of the rain!' said Lizzie.

The officer came through the door and took off his outer coat and cap, leaving them in the utility room as even in the short distance from the car to the door, he had got soaked. He had to bend slightly as he walked into the office to save from banging his head. As they faced each other he spoke softly and gravely.

'Mrs Tennyson? Are you alone, or is there anyone else here?' he asked gently.

'Well, Bert my colleague is in the bar and my son is asleep upstairs, at least I hope he is asleep. What is it, what's wrong – is it my husband, I was expecting him home before now, he is rather late and the weather is terrible. He hasn't had an accident has he? Please just tell me.' Lizzie felt alarm rising inside her.

'I am sorry,' he paused. 'I have some bad news for you. Why don't we sit down? Can I just check the registration number of a car registered in the name of Mr Richard Tennyson – your husband I believe?' Lizzie confirmed the number and waited in silence, full of impending doom.

'You see, there has been an accident,' said Gary slowly. 'Well, somehow the vehicle left the road along the Overton Pass.' He swallowed and Lizzie saw the Adam's apple in his neck bob up and down. What a daft thing to notice she thought later.

She sank down onto one of the office chairs and clutched her stomach.

'Is he okay?' she asked tentatively, even as she did so she felt she knew the answer to that question. Gary Carmichael sat down on the chair opposite her. He continued in his quiet calm way.

'Emergency Services co-ordinated the recovery, they managed to get him out of the vehicle but his injuries were severe. I am so sorry, he was pronounced dead on arrival at hospital.'

Lizzie could not believe what she was hearing.

'But how could that happen? I don't understand – Richard was a good driver. What on earth was he doing driving along the Overton Pass; it is not on his route home?' She shook her head as if trying to get rid of the information she had just been given.

'We don't know anything for sure yet, forensic officers are at the site now and we will know more when the car has been examined,' said the officer softly. 'Now is there anyone I can call for you? You really shouldn't be alone.'

'Oh my goodness, I can't take this in – I feel like I'm in a dream,' muttered Lizzie. 'But no, no I will ring my parents in the morning – there is no point in worrying them tonight – I don't want my father driving in this weather. Richard's parents live in Spain near to his sister and her family, so I will need to contact them too. I really need to be with him, see him. Where has he been taken?' Lizzie pulled her hands through her hair; she was shaking and could hardly speak coherently as her mouth felt numb and her tongue didn't seem to fit properly.

'I will drive you to the hospital now if that's okay with you? And we will contact your parents; leave it to us,' said Gary with calm efficiency, as he turned to the radio device attached to the front of his uniform.

Lizzie just sat back and let events take over. Bert had clearly realised that something was wrong and had rung Ruby his wife and Maggie his daughter, both of whom appeared at the back door, soaking wet and panting as they had run through the village as soon as they had taken the call.

Maggie went through to the bar to help her father and Ruby took charge of Lizzie as if she was a small child. Getting her coat and sending her off with the police officer. She assured Lizzie that she would stay with Alex until whatever time Lizzie got back from the hospital.

*

When Lizzie finally crawled into her empty lonely bed in the middle of the night, having been tucked in by the ever attentive Ruby, she curled up in a ball and sobbed into her pillow. She cried until she could produce no more tears and her teeth chattered together as she leaned over to hug Richard's pillow.

The staff had been very kind at the hospital. Everyone had treated her with the utmost respect and compassion. She hoped it had all been a terrible mistake but there was no doubt; Richard was dead.

After she had been driven back home, Ruby had arranged for the duty GP to come to give Lizzie a sleeping draught; she did not actually want to sleep, she just wanted to wrap Richard in her arms and tell him she loved him. She could not even remember their last conversation. She had been in a hurry and did not even think she had kissed him, however perfunctorily. She would never get the opportunity again.

Poor Richard he had been so alive, so full of ideas – this did not need to have happened. Life was so cruel sometimes.

*

Lizzie had no idea how she got through the following few weeks – she felt dazed, like she was watching someone else performing the daily tasks of living. She tried to keep things as normal as possible for Alex as uppermost in her mind was her desire to protect her son from as much pain as possible.

Some mornings she awoke and for a split second did not remember what had happened. Then the awful truth hit her like a sledge hammer ramming into her chest.

Things proceeded as smoothly as they could. There had to be a post mortem and an inquest of course. A police report revealed that Richard had been travelling too fast for the road conditions that evening. The brakes were found to be faulty due to wear and tear and would certainly have failed the MOT which was due at the end of the month.

The question of what Richard was doing driving along the Overton Pass was explained by Lizzie who after a day or two, remembered a conversation from a few weeks previously, when Richard had said he would go over to The Swan at Hangmere, when he got a chance, as he had heard good reports about the place. His business brain was always tuned into ideas and innovations from any source available.

A verdict of accidental death was recorded by the coroner.

*

His funeral attracted a huge turnout. Mainly they were there to pay their respects to Lizzie, whom everyone cared deeply about.

'I could take him or leave him,' one villager was heard to say, 'but I have a lot of time for her, I do hope she stays, having her around the village has made such a difference'.

In the weeks that followed, unbeknown to Lizzie, an action plan was launched by the villagers to try to convince her to stay. The pub was as packed as ever. Lifts were organised for Alex to go to and from school to relieve her of that burden and every able-bodied man for miles around offered to change a barrel "any time you like". She was heartened by this, but mostly she was grateful to Bert and Ruby who took her under their wings like she was one of their own.

Ruby seemed to be there every time Lizzie turned round; sorting some washing, bringing back some ironing, making her take a break, feeding Alex and helping him with his homework as best she could.

Thankfully Richard had bullied Lizzie into taking her publican's licence, not that she could really see the need to do so, but he had insisted and it was easier to pacify him than to protest. However, it did feel strange and rather final to see her name replacing his above the door once the transfer had been completed.

She felt a mixture of sadness and trepidation as she realised that little by little Richard's presence was being removed from the pub and their lives.

Maggie became a fixture behind the bar, freeing Lizzie up to concentrate on the food theoretically, but she found her heart was not in it and employed a nice lady from the village to do lunches and curtailed the evening menu to three items each day, the preparation of which she could cope with.

Time marched relentlessly on and after a while she started to get cross with herself – she really must stop being so pathetic. She attended a concert at Alex's school. People smiled at her kindly and she wondered if she looked as pitiful as she felt.

She began to wonder if she would really enjoy anything ever again. "Anhedonia" the GP had called it – the inability to experience pleasure – yes that was her, anhedonic – if that was actually a word.

Maybe she should get involved with the amateur dramatic society once more; they seemed a bit directionless without her input. The pantomime production had been cancelled after Richard's accident. She felt that she should help out even if only backstage in a small way with the latest play; sadly though motivation eluded her.

Richard's parents and sister had been devastated by the news of his death and spent a few weeks with her and Alex after the funeral before returning to Spain, with an offer to visit whenever she wanted and to stay for as long as she liked. However she could not leave the pub for an extended period of time; if she left it would be for good.

Her parents had taken to turning up uninvited on a regular basis and during one particularly tempestuous visit, after quite a lot of general nit-picking, her mother announced that Lizzie should sell up and move in with them. They had ended up having an almighty argument towards the end of their stay.

Lizzie tried to remember what her mother had said. Something like, "…put all this silly pub nonsense behind you; it was what Richard wanted, not you. You need to think about yourself and poor Alex now." That was her mother – tactful as ever! She was still muttering and shaking her head as Lizzie's father bundled her into the car for the return journey to Bournemouth.

In fact Lizzie was quite grateful to her parents as it had made her see things a bit more clearly. By getting cross with her mother, she realised with a clarity sadly lacking for months that she didn't want to go to Bournemouth or Spain, so by default they should stay put in Blenthorne if they could manage it.

With a sense of determination she hadn't experienc since Richard died, she realised she was not ready to throv the towel yet.

Alex was getting older and very keen to help her a⸱ as he could. They had a chat and in a very mature w said he would support any decision she made. So it w – Blenthorne was their home and in Blenthorne ⸱ stay. She just had to put her mind to planning hc achieve this.

However, as is often the way in life when ⸱ somewhere a window opens.

35

Chapter 3

Jim – 1994

In the aftermath of Richard's death, Lizzie seemed to alternate between manic activity and apathy. At times she threw herself into the running of the pub; no amount of persuasion on the part of Bert, Ruby or Maggie would stop her and at other times she found she didn't really want to get out of bed.

The GP said this was all part of the grieving process and that she could have some medication and maybe some counselling. What she really wanted was Richard and their old life back. After a while she wondered if she was in danger of becoming a professional widow surrounded by a perpetual air of sadness. However, bit by bit things improved and she found at times she was even sharing a joke in the bar with a customer.

The ideas for the redevelopment of the barn had had to be shelved and she was no further forward with the redecoration of the two bars, other than a quick coat of emulsion on the walls – "a lick and a promise", as her nan would have said. However the clientele had stayed loyal and they seemed to be attracting as many customers as when Richard was alive.

Bert was as always her greatest support and biggest critic; giving her a pep talk when needed and proverbial kick up the backside if he felt that was more appropriate. He had completely given up his painting and decorating business to concentrate on helping her, bless him.

Maggie was happily married to Carl who worked away from home, so it suited everyone for her to continue to live with her parents in the village so that they could save enough money to buy a place of their own in due course.

Life rolled on and the passing months turned into years without drama or crisis and things settled into a comfortable familiar routine.

Unfortunately Lizzie was shaken back to the harsh realities of life one overcast Tuesday morning towards the end of June just after dropping Alex and a neighbour's daughter at school. Maggie appeared at the door.

'Oh there you are; where's your father? Busy day today, brewery delivery and I have a meeting with the accountant later. Do you want to make a start in the kitchen and I'll concentrate on ...' Lizzie stopped as she saw that Maggie was trying to stop herself from crying. 'Whatever is it?' asked Lizzie with a sense of foreboding.

'It's Dad, oh heavens Lizzie, he has had a heart attack I think – he just keeled over in the kitchen when he went downstairs to make Mum an early morning cup of tea. They have taken him to Carlisle. It looks bad, I'm not sure he will make it ... I wanted to come and tell you myself rather than ringing.' She dissolved into sobs and nose blowing.

'Oh my goodness – Maggie I am so sorry, that's terrible news ... Okay, we'll close the pub today – no arguments, we need to go – I'll just get my bag. We need to get to the hospital. Um, I had better ring the brewery and the accountant,' said Lizzie, putting on the practical head which she had not needed to use for so long. Bert and his family had been there for that ever since Richard had died.

She taped a handwritten note to the main entrance of the pub stating that the Blenny was closed for the day as Bert was in hospital. News would be given out as soon as they knew anything.

It had started to drizzle and the drive to the hospital was tortuous; thankfully there were no holdups on the way but the journey seemed to take an age. They drove more or less in silence as both were caught up in their thoughts and fears of "what if" as they watched the windscreen wipers clear the rain in a gentle rhythm.

Once they arrived they were shown into a waiting area where they found Ruby and also Maggie's brother Tim who had joined them from Keswick. Lizzie was unsure whether to stay or not, wondering if she was intruding on a family's private suffering, of which really she should have no involvement. Ruby told her she wanted her to stay.

'You're family,' she said firmly.

So Lizzie and the Bumsteads sat drinking coffee and exchanging the occasional small banal comment for the next two hours.

Finally Ruby was allowed to see Bert after the registrar explained that tests had indicated he had suffered an ST segment elevation myocardial infarction. In simple terms the doctor explained, it meant that he had experienced a prolonged blockage of the blood supply to his heart caused by a clot – a heart attack in common language. He had been administered clot busting drugs and currently he was in a critical although stable condition.

Ruby made her way to his bedside and the others all breathed a small sigh of relief, an unspoken acknowledgement of the fact that he was still with them.

Lizzie hung around at the hospital for several hours. Alex had been collected by the mother of a friend who was giving him his tea. Tim assured her he would see both his mum and sister home safely. Maggie's husband Carl was on his way back from Aberdeenshire and would be with them later that night.

Lizzie drove back towards home and could not help selfishly thinking about how Bert's heart attack would affect her and the running of the pub. This could mean the end for her in her struggle to be independent and manage alone, because the harsh reality was that she was not managing alone – dear, kind, big, dependable Bert had always been there for her, even if he was rather lumbering and a bit slow; he was part of the place and part of her life.

Best case scenario, he might recover sufficiently to return to work but it would be ages – months maybe. It was possible that he would never be able to do anything other than light duties. Worse case, he would not recover, or if he did, he would be incapacitated and unable to work at all.

After collecting Alex and returning home, Lizzie realised she had to make a decision – accept defeat, sell up and move to

Bournemouth as her mother suggested or find someone to help run the pub, at least in the short term.

As she prepared their supper she made up her mind to speak to Maggie tomorrow, as sensitively as possible, to tell her they needed to find a replacement for Bert as she was not ready to leave Blenthorne yet.

She taped an updated bulletin on the pub door and then she and Alex had a quiet peaceful evening watching television and eating chocolate, which was such a treat for them. Even if she had an evening off, they could still hear the hubbub of voices and noise from downstairs and the commotion of closing time.

Speaking to Maggie next day was easier than she had imagined; in fact Maggie broached the subject first.

'We are going to need some help Lizzie,' she said calmly. 'We can't do this alone, Dad may be laid up for ages – they are talking about him staying in hospital for at least seven days and then off to rehab; he may even need a coronary bypass operation in the longer term. No, we are definitely going to need a man.'

They both looked at each other and laughed, immediately feeling guilty for doing so.

'Shall we stipulate in the advert that any applicants will need to perfect the technique of wiping their nose without the use of a hanky?' said Maggie keeping her face straight.

'Oh Maggie don't,' said Lizzie as she went to the drawer in the office to find some paper and a pen.

They sat together over a cup of coffee compiling an advert for the local paper and employment centre, having decided to do that prior to going to an agency, as it would obviously be much cheaper.

They would see what came of it.

*

Jim Lockwood sat in a small café near one of the museums in Keswick, he had looked through the local paper several times; there was one job in particular that caught his eye.

"Full-time bartender wanted for rural inn, experience preferred and flexibility essential" – could he do it he wondered?

He had some experience of bar work, but then he had experience of lots of types of casual work. He had been a cleaner, cashier, car valet, kitchen assistant, road sweeper – you name it and he had done it – over the past few years. He hadn't been able to stay in each job for any length of time as the demons always found him again. He picked up his coffee cup and brought it unsteadily to his lips.

He had ended up in Keswick by accident really. He and his older sister Sheila had been born in south east London where they had had a happy childhood. His father was a chauffeur and his mother a full time housewife. When Jim was ten his mother died suddenly as a result of a brain aneurysm; two years later his father met Jackie whom he later married. She had two children of a similar age to him and Sheila. Inevitably there was friction when they all lived together in one small cramped house.

Jackie had wanted to move back to the north east where her family came from, not only that but house prices were cheaper and they could obtain the much needed space they craved. Without discussing it with either Jim or Sheila, his father had agreed to the move.

After a few years of fairly dysfunctional living within their reconstituted family, Sheila met and married Steve who came from Darlington. Jim had joined the army, married Sarah and moved wherever he was stationed. When he had left the army and his marriage ended, he had gravitated back to be near Sheila and her family.

Thinking of the army immediately made his thoughts turn to his time in combat.

He thought back to his mates, the ambush ... His eyes were starting to blink rapidly as he broke into a sweat. His heart began to pound inside his chest. Remember the technique; remember the coping mechanisms; slow down the eye movement; breathe steadily; get the heart rate back to normal. That was it – yes, he could do it if he tried hard. He placed the cup back in the saucer with a slightly shaky hand.

He realised he had scrunched the job section of the paper into a ball and it was damp with sweat from his hands; he smoothed it out and looked again at the advert that had particularly caught his attention. Maybe an inn in a country environment would suit him, if he could make a good enough impression. Tranquil surroundings might well help him to stay on an even keel. He was making progress he was sure of it. He just needed to hold it all together.

He finished his cold coffee and on walking out of the door made towards the phone box on the corner, summoning up the courage to make the call.

*

Lizzie wondered what this chap would turn out to be like, he had sounded quite nervous on the phone. Maggie was going to be around and she would get her opinion before making a decision.

The general response had not been encouraging; the salary was not particularly attractive, so maybe it was to be expected. Lizzie was just thinking she would have to go to an agency when the phone had rung and this chap – what was his name – Jim something, Lockwood that was it – had enquired if the vacancy was still available. They had arranged for him to come along today for an informal interview.

Lizzie looked at her watch as she waited by the door.

*

Jim had been up at the crack of dawn. He had put out his clean clothes the night before, so that everything was ready for the morning and he would not need to rush. He had showered and shaved but couldn't bring himself to eat any breakfast. He had checked on the buses and found the nearest stop was in Rowendale a couple of miles away; he didn't want to be late, so he got the first one of the day and consequently arrived over an hour early. Now he stood outside the Blenthorne Inn wondering if he had could see this through after all.

Would he have the courage to knock on the door when the time came? What if he were asked to do a trial shift and spilt the drinks or broke the glasses, what if he reacted to loud noises, as sometimes happened and he found himself screaming and shaking against a wall – maybe he should just go back to Keswick …

He well remembered Sarah's reaction to his outbursts; at first she had been gentle and sympathetic, then she had tried to reason with him, at times she got cross and finally she admitted she could not deal with it any longer.

Sadly their marriage became a part of the statistics which demonstrated that war veterans cannot always make an easy transition to civilian life and their nearest and dearest suffer as much as they do.

He did not blame her; no-one could have lived with him as he was. He had had professional support after his honourable discharge from the army; they had even given him a label – Post Traumatic Stress Disorder.

So Sarah had left him and now he and his PTSD lived together as best they could. The question was, could he control his anxieties sufficiently to get through this interview and if he managed that, could he actually do the job adequately?

It was time. He straightened his tie and walked towards the door, now or never, just try your best he told himself as he listened to his heart thudding hard against his ribcage. He knocked tentatively on the door.

The door opened and he was greeted by a woman roughly his own age or slightly older he judged; she was quite tall and had a strong build. She had nice teeth and a pleasant face. Her eyes shone out from under her dark fringe and her smile was gentle and encouraging. She was wearing a blue sweatshirt and black jeans.

'Hello, I'm Lizzie Tennyson,' she said, 'you must be Jim? Do come in, it's very nice to meet you.'

Jim swallowed and nodded, smiling back nervously.

*

Lizzie saw before her a chap probably in his mid-thirties who was just a little over six feet tall with a broad frame and closely cropped light brownish hair, balding from the front. His face looked tired and careworn. He was wearing a smart pale coloured jacket with a black shirt and black and yellow striped tie and dark tailored trousers.

He held out his hand in response to hers and as she took it, she was pleased to note that this formal ritual had not been preceded by any contact with his nose and the back of his hand appeared completely free of any residue.

He had a nice firm handshake; that was a good start thought Lizzie, not at all displeased with what she had seen so far. Although the choice of tie suggested there was probably no Mrs Lockwood.

'I'm Jim Lockwood, thank you for agreeing to see me Mrs Tennyson.' From his slightly faltering tone, Lizzie wondered if Jim was trying to engender a degree of confidence into his voice that he did not feel.

'Lizzie, no-one calls me Mrs Tennyson!' she said brightly. She could not put her finger on why, but she wanted to put this slightly awkward anxious man at ease as best she could. She took him into the office and offered him the seat opposite hers.

'So tell me about yourself Jim,' Lizzie started pleasantly as she leaned forward in her chair.

She noted that Jim kept it brief as he skimmed over his military service and outlined his subsequent employment.

'Rather a lot of jobs Jim. Any particular reason why you travelled around and have never found anything that suited you for long?' asked Lizzie, crossing her legs and looking at him enquiringly.

Jim hesitated and appeared more nervous than previously.

'I… well, I haven't always been able to stay in jobs for long … My, um, my mental health sometimes lets me down …' his voice trailed off.

Lizzie looked at him with her head slightly to one side.

'How about I put the kettle on? I think things are always easier with the aid of a nice cup of tea, don't you?' Lizzie's heart suddenly went out to the sad defeated looking man before her.

Jim looked at her with what she perceived to be a degree of relief as he sighed and visibly relaxed a little. Over the next half hour with the assistance of his cup of tea, a refill and several biscuits, he divulged details about his time in the army, the PTSD and his marriage break up. Lizzie appreciated his honesty but did wonder if he was trying to talk himself into or out of the job.

*

When Jim finally finished speaking he became aware that he was sitting forward on the chair leaning towards Lizzie and telling her how much he wanted to take control of his life – he suddenly realised that it was true – he really did want to move forward and make a fresh start. If nothing else came of today, at least he could take that out of the encounter. However, it suddenly registered that Lizzie was talking to him and he was not concentrating properly.

'...we need help because my regular barman Bert is unwell ... usually about half past six when the first regular arrives ... steady stream after that and of course we never know quite what will happen in the lounge bar, we do food and at this time of year, things are getting busier as the walkers begin to take their holidays. I would need you to take charge of the brewery deliveries and do you know how to change a barrel, if not, don't worry I can show you ... And of course the cleaning of the pipework is essential, but again not a problem if you are happy to learn – from what you have heard so far Jim, do you think this is somewhere you would like to be or maybe you might find it a bit on the quiet side? Do you have a clean driving licence? It would be helpful if you could go to the wholesalers sometimes. Is it the type of job you are after? What I am trying to say is – would you take the job if I offered it to you?'

Lizzie blinked as she looked at Jim who gulped and stared at her. She had asked him about a dozen questions without giving him any time to respond – he felt rather bewildered, which should he try to answer first? Maybe he should just get up and run away. However, he was quite impressed with himself when he managed to remain seated and he hoped his expression did not give away the sense of alarm he was feeling.

'You would really give me a chance?' he said finally with disbelief, 'after what I have told you about my mental health problems and my past.'

'Everyone deserves a chance Jim. Maggie and I need help here. We don't know what will happen with Bert, but unless or until he is back to full strength, we can't manage – so how about it? If you are as willing as you say, we will give you a trial if you will give us one.'

Jim could not believe what he was hearing. He did not want to appear over-eager.

'Well, yes that would be great, if you are happy to give me some training as I haven't worked in a bar for a while but I'm prepared to do anything you want, to be of any service I can – thank you Lizzie.'

His heart leapt in elation as he realised he had just got a job!

*

For a brief moment Lizzie thought Jim was going to kiss her, the unbridled joy on his face was a sight to behold; she found herself laughing as they shook hands, making plans before they did so for Jim to bring back all his documentation and have a training session the following day.

She saw him out of the door and as he looked back she smiled and waved. Her heart felt lighter than for a long time as she closed the door. Just good to get a barman she told herself, nothing more.

After Jim had left Lizzie walked into the bar area where Maggie was just about to open up and Lizzie could see a youngish couple sitting on the wall outside, waiting to be let in – when the clientele were that keen they normally took bets as to whether it was their warm welcome or the toilets they were really after.

'So, then Mrs – someone has brought a smile to your face and a spring to your step – I thought you mentioned you were going to let me see him for my opinion?' said Maggie in mock accusatory style.

'Oh yes, I did sorry. It was just, well we got talking and all was going well and … anyway you can meet him tomorrow as I said we would give him a trial, well not really a trial, more of a um, well a training session … sort of thing …'

Lizzie realised she was blushing slightly as Maggie nodded and grinned, her tongue firmly placed in her right cheek.

'What?' said Lizzie as nonchalantly as she could manage.

'Oh nothing!' grinned Maggie, 'already looking forward to tomorrow, as I suspect you are!' She ducked as Lizzie hurled a rolled up tea towel at her.

Lizzie smiled as she got ready for bed that night; she really hoped that Jim would work out. He seemed strong and capable but somehow just a bit lost. She didn't think she had conducted the interview very well; she had talked far too much and got rather flustered if she was honest. But he had seemed so pleased when she had offered him the job – his reaction was touching. To think, she had actually thought he was going to step closer and kiss her; she blushed as she suddenly realised that she would not have minded too much if he had.

*

Jim was also going to bed at his B&B in Keswick. Today had gone better than he could possibly have hoped.

The place seemed nice, fairly informal and Lizzie appeared pleasant and friendly, if a bit loud and excitable. He hoped he could make a good impression tomorrow when he would be training with the barmaid – what was her name? He couldn't remember. Tomorrow could be a turning point in his life he thought as he turned off the radio and the light.

Little did he know how right he was.

Chapter 4

Life in Blenthorne – 1994/6

Jim had arrived punctually for his training the next day. Maggie noticed with a smile that Lizzie had let her hair out of the confines of the usual rubber band and it was hanging loosely around her shoulders, all washed and bouncy. She also seemed to be wearing a bit more make up than usual. No old jogging bottoms this morning either – smart jeans, figure hugging and flattering and yes, Maggie sniffed the air subtly – Lizzie was wearing her favourite perfume. Well good for her thought Maggie, about time she took a bit of interest in herself. Nothing to do with Jim, Maggie was sure!

Maggie found Jim a willing and eager pupil behind the bar who was not afraid of hard work. He asked a lot of questions and was clearly a bit scared of making mistakes. However with Maggie's gentle and kind instruction he soon found that his confidence grew. He picked up the workings of the till quickly and without many mistakes.

Over the next few weeks the ladies noticed with delight that he was quick to volunteer for any job, however menial or unpleasant. To keep costs down, Lizzie and Maggie did the cleaning between them, so it was with tremendous pleasure – not to say relief – that they agreed readily to Jim's suggestion that he could take over this task; but Lizzie did say it would ruin Maggie's day if she could not complain about the things some people thought appropriate to shove down a toilet.

*

Jim seemed to be adapting well to his new surroundings and appeared more contented and settled as each day passed. He had found a B&B in the village which was convenient for working at the Blenny. His landlady was an elderly lady by the name of Naomi Watts who had lived nearby all her life, having been born into a farming family and staying put until she was forced by failing health to surrender the lease.

She had moved to a cottage in the village and took in lodgers and tourists. It was not salubrious but it was reasonably clean and above all fairly cheap. She did fuss a bit and often called Jim "Cyril", the name of her brother who was killed in action during World War II. Jim found he was doing a few little jobs here and there for Naomi, who was always grateful but never suggested a reduction in his rent.

Lizzie became aware that Jim was spending less and less time at his lodgings as he got to work early each day and often they would share a cup of coffee after closing time before he left for the night. Lizzie had tried to put up his wages as the additional work he was putting in had not gone unnoticed by her. However he refused to take anything more than payment for his contracted hours, saying that he was just happy to be doing something which he enjoyed so much and was grateful for the opportunity. She remembered he had also mentioned an army pension, so she supposed he was doing okay financially.

Lizzie knew that Jim still had a few bad days with the old anxieties trying to intrude into his life, but by and large, she thought he was doing well. He was still in touch with his counsellor who apparently seemed very pleased with his progress. On the bad days, Lizzie left him alone and if he did not feel up to doing two shifts behind the bar, she always suggested he have time off. He normally refused and busied himself in the kitchen, preparing salads and washing up.

Lizzie was pleased that Jim got on well with the customers, both regular and visiting. He had a natural spontaneous manner. She could not help but make the comparison with Richard who could turn the charm on and off at the press of a button. Jim was different – he was a genuinely nice amiable chap. She congratulated herself on being a good judge of character and felt he really was an asset to the business.

She thought the village suited him; she noticed that he had got to know quite a few people in the time he had been there and had made a point of remembering the regulars' names and gave them a friendly greeting upon arrival. She also noticed that whenever anyone offered to buy him a drink he never accepted anything more than a lager shandy, which he may or may not drink later in the evening. She was pleased to note that he never took advantage of anyone's generosity, knowing how financially tight things were for many local people; in fact more than once she noticed that he bought some of the regulars a drink in return.

Gradually as his confidence grew, Lizzie invited him along to things she was involved with. "This is Jim", she would say; with no further explanation and she felt sure many people who didn't know better, probably thought they were an item. She realised this was a bit presumptive but he seemed quite comfortable.

*

For his part, Jim felt Lizzie had been tremendously kind to him and he was genuinely very fond of her; his sense of wellbeing had increased immeasurably since he had started his job. He liked the work and found he was able to help Lizzie in all sorts of ways and she often sought his opinion when a decision needed to be made.

In particular he had built up a good relationship with Alex. Jim helped him with homework, had a kick about with a football, taught him to tie sailor's knots and make balloon animals. He had enjoyed a good relationship with his own father until he had remarried and Jim realised it must be tough for Lizzie trying to bring up her son alone. If he could play a small part in helping fill a void in Alex's life, then he was happy to do so.

He took Alex to rugby and football training, more often than Lizzie and he was always happy to help out during training sessions, frequently getting as filthy as Alex after acting as linesman as and when needed. Lizzie was never cross about the state they came home in and told him as well as Alex to pop their clothes in the washing machine. He really did feel very much part of the family at times.

One day recently Alex had come home and said that his youth adventure group needed some trustworthy adults to help with trips and would he be okay with that. Jim found himself incredibly proud to be asked and after checking with Lizzie, agreed readily. Mostly the excursions were in the daytime but occasionally they did an overnight camp on the fells. Jim was able to show the boys some of his survival techniques – he found this very cathartic; bringing back memories of his service days in a positive way.

The latest thing was a "dads and lads" cricket match against Rowendale. Jim did wonder if he had bitten off a bit more than he could chew this time, as cricket was not really his forte. However, he said would give it a go. He would need to go into Keswick or maybe Carlisle to get some appropriate footwear and a bat – pads and ball were apparently provided.

He had also just been asked by the local volunteer fell rescue team if he would consider becoming a member. Some of the team drank in the Blenny and one day one just threw the idea at him casually.

'How about joining us Jim?'

He was quite keen on the idea as again it would give him something really positive to do with the skills he had learned during his years as a soldier and hopefully he would not witness anything like the sights he had seen in the theatres of war. He had been told that most likely he would encounter nothing worse than a broken ankle. He said he would need to talk to Lizzie though to see if she would mind. Naturally, she thought the idea was an excellent one and gave him her full support, as somehow he knew she would.

Little by little it seemed he was being absorbed into the community and a warm feeling of security was gradually enveloping him like a gentle embrace.

*

One particular day a few months later Lizzie smiled as she watched Alex and Jim come in from the garden; some sort of dispute seemed to have erupted regarding the off-side rule and apparently Jim's last goal was disallowed.

'Hands!' she shouted when she heard them coming through the utility room, 'and shoes off please.'

'In trouble again Alex; entirely your fault!' said Jim as he turned on the hot tap and picked up the soap.

'My fault – what about you; you were first through the door!' said Alex as he grabbed the soap from Jim's hand.

How she loved to hear the happy banter, of which sometimes they allowed her to be part – although usually she was the butt of the jokes.

She remembered the time before Jim came into her life – almost another world it now seemed. She didn't realise how many balls she was trying to juggle at once. The burden had originally been borne by Bert until he became ill. Jim then appeared and had gently and slowly taken many of the daily tasks of running the pub from her. She really did not know what she would do without him.

Bert was still making steady progress and was now back doing a few light duties. Mainly though he just sat on a stool behind the bar and chatted to the regulars. Good for business Jim said; they got on extremely well, so much better than Bert's relationship with Richard. When tourists arrived it was great for them to see a bit of old authentic rural life. They then had the choice; they could go into the lounge bar or mingle with the regulars in the public bar. Over time they found this worked well, as often all male climbing and walking groups liked the macho ambiance they found by joining in with the locals. So different to what Richard had wanted to do – knocking the two bars into one and putting locks on the toilets indeed!

Even with Jim's salary to take into account, the business was doing well. She had employed Tim, Bert's son from Keswick to spruce up the two bars, as Bert really could not do much in the way of decorating since his heart attack.

The dark oppressive decor of the public bar had already been replaced with a lighter shade of emulsion on the walls to maximise the feeling of space – this was re-done and looked far smarter than the hurried coat they had slapped on previously. They had kept the brasses and plaques and Lizzie had bought a few old books from a jumble sale to stand on the window sills. The regulars were encouraged to have their own personalised tankards if they so wished, to really make them feel at home and these hung in splendour from the top shelf behind the bar. She had had new flagstone floors laid in both bars with rugs in the lounge bar.

She was very pleased with the overall effect but had to forcefully stop herself from thinking of Richard and his trip to Carlisle on that fateful day whenever anyone complimented her on her choice of flooring. She had kept close to the original colour scheme of off white in the lounge bar and when money permitted she changed the furnishings and incorporated comfortable leather sofas as well as some upright chairs in complimentary fabrics.

With Jim's encouragement Lizzie thoughts had turned to the barn conversion idea again and she had approached an architect recommended by Tim Bumstead, something Richard had planned to do but unfortunately not had time to put in place. Once completed the plans were submitted for the necessary council approval and thankfully this turned out to be a fairly painless process.

She and Maggie had hatched a plot to tempt Carl, Maggie's husband, home from Aberdeen. He already helped out behind the bar and in the kitchen when he was not on shift – he did six days on and six off as a head chef on an oil rig. His food went down well with their diners and Maggie had asked if there would be any chance that Lizzie might employ him when the restaurant was open. That way he could return home; they had saved enough to get a mortgage for their own place and would no longer need to live with Bert and Ruby. Lizzie liked this idea a lot; keeping everything in the family as she thought of it.

*

Whenever Carl was home and able to help Maggie and Bert, Lizzie allowed herself to be dragged away from the village by Jim, which was something that she and Richard virtually never did. He was always so busy with plans and business ideas and meetings, so whenever they had any time off, it seemed they never spent it together. In fact it had seemed to Lizzie, the more she immersed herself in village life, the more impervious Richard became.

She and Jim climbed and walked and talked and had pub lunches – busman's holidays as they liked to think of it. Jim said it was always good to see what the opposition was offering in the way of food and hospitality. Lizzie shivered as she remembered Richard had been doing something similar on the night he died. Another shadow from the past – don't think of it.

They walked in all weathers, preferring the sun but making do with the rain, mist and fog and indeed sometimes almost blizzard conditions. They tackled Coniston Old Man – Lizzie was amazed to ascend for what seemed like miles only to be confronted with a large rusting crane-like structure looming above them, left over from the days of copper and slate mining. She understood that local livelihood relied on mining in the area in years gone by but she felt this stark reminder was like an ugly great carbuncle detracting from the magnificence of the mountain. Jim, ever practical, said it would cost a fortune to dismantle and remove it. Lots of people probably felt the same way about its aesthetic appearance but it did not stop them arriving in droves to attempt the ascent.

She had the same feeling when they climbed High Street, only to find four-by-four wheeled vehicles on the top. Apparently it had been a thoroughfare in Roman times, linking the forts between Brougham and Ambleside, so it was practically a motorway! There was no clear way round the mountain, so the ever resourceful Romans had done the obvious thing and gone over the top.

They did the whole of the Fairfield Horseshoe, but not in one day – Lizzie drew the line at that when Jim told her how many miles it would be.

She loved being on the fells, in particular the wonderful scrambling that ascending Cat Bells offered with the reward at the top being the stunning views offered by Derwentwater on a clear day. She had a soft spot for Dollywaggon Pike with Grisedale Tarn nestling at the bottom – however her favourite fell walk was not much of a climb at all. It was a circular route which took them across open moorland to Dock Tarn, near the summit of Great Crag, midway between Watendlath, the Stonewaith Valley and Borrowdale.

As they walked they talked and Jim told Lizzie something of his life in the army, his friends and comrades, both alive and fallen. Briefly without going into too much detail, he told her about the day that changed his life and the ambush which took the lives of several of his colleagues.

Whenever he mentioned the past, Lizzie never pressed him to say more than he wanted but listened quietly as he divulged thoughts and feelings that clearly at times still troubled him.

The first time they stood together by the shoreline at Dock Tarn, Jim finally told Lizzie about Sarah, his ex-wife.

They had been happy together; they had known each other from school and had discussed his desire to join the army before they got engaged. He had applied with her blessing and support. Although she worried about him when he was on deployment, she never complained or criticised him for the choice he had made.

His mental health issues after his discharge had knocked them both for six. Bless her, Sarah had tried to help him through his problems but at that time he could not let anyone into his own private nightmare. After struggling on for about a year, they had decided to call it a day. Well, Sarah had to be more precise. She had told Jim she could not help him anymore and she felt he clearly no longer loved her.

'I will never stop loving her actually, I just couldn't show it,' Jim told Lizzie as they walked along by the quiet waters of the tarn.

Lizzie saw some ducks bobbing their heads down into the water making small silent ripples as her brain absorbed what Jim had just said. She had heard of the saying "blood runs cold" and if she was honest, that was the exact feeling she had at that moment as an icy feeling penetrated deeply to her core.

'I see,' she said tentatively, thinking maybe it would best to try to retain a little bit of dignity by not saying anything that would give her feelings away.

'What I mean is, I suppose, I don't blame her for needing to get away. No-one could have coped with my mood swings and self-loathing. I was no longer the person I was before the Gulf, the person she wanted me to be, so our life together could not continue at that point – our relationship became, what is the word – dysfunctional.'

'The thing is Lizzie, I felt guilty for being alive; crazy though that may sound but nothing Sarah or anyone else could do would change that. Somehow over time and since meeting you with your kindness and care, I have managed to get my head above water again and keep it there.'

He paused for a moment.

'You and Alex have taken me into your lives and I am happier now than I ever thought I could be again. My goodness – that is the longest monologue I have delivered in my entire life – but it is true, I am not sure what I would do without you.'

Jim leaned forward and kissed Lizzie gently on the cheek and she stroked his face with her gloved hand. As they walked on, they linked arms and smiled at each other.

Lizzie felt overwhelmed with emotion; she acknowledged to herself that she loved Jim very much; hopefully maybe he was beginning to feel something more than just gratitude for her. The ice running through her veins was slowly replaced by a gentle warm glow as the drizzle started to fall and they trudged towards a welcome cup of tea at Watendlath.

*

Over the coming months all Lizzie's dreams came true as their relationship gradually blossomed from caring friendship to a deeper unspoken commitment to each other. By the following summer Jim had traded Naomi Watts' dubious hospitality for the tenderness and love of Lizzie and Alex's home over the Blenny.

'First job, with your approval,' said Jim as he looked towards Lizzie, 'are those blinking wonky cupboards. I have looked at them for months every time we had coffee together up here but I think it really is time we did something about them! Alex, how about we go to the DIY shop in Keswick tomorrow morning? Is that alright with you?'

'Fine with me,' said Lizzie as she walked into the kitchen. 'In a strange sort of way, I think I will miss them a bit.'

'Can't really see what's wrong with them myself, but if you want to, yes I'll go with you,' said Alex, who was still trying hard to perfect his nonchalant sulky teenage persona. However the affection between them was clearly genuine, so it amused Lizzie to see that he kept forgetting to be monosyllabic and disinterested when he was around Jim.

Jim, with a bit of help from Alex and quite a lot from Tim Bumstead, transformed the kitchen in the flat in a matter of weeks. New white cupboards, which all matched, were attached to the walls, and aligned with the aid of a spirit level. These were complemented by new work surfaces and the grubby orange blind gave way to a sleek slatted wooden one. A new white oak lacquered floor replaced the old torn red linoleum.

After that they refurnished the lounge area in subtle coffee and creams and bought new leather sofas and two occasional tables on which they stood lamps. Matching blinds covered the windows with drapes to the sides. The large orange flowered wallpaper was consigned to history but Lizzie kept a small piece as she thought that not even she would remember just how truly awful it actually was without a tangible reminder. With the old blue carpet removed and a new tan coloured short twist pile replacement in situ, the makeover of the room was complete.

The two bedrooms in the apartment also benefited from a coat of emulsion and seemed transformed. Lizzie planned to choose some material for the bedroom curtains next time she went to Carlisle. The pale blue bathroom suite would have to do for now and they also promised themselves they would do something about the avocado en suites in the guests' rooms when time and money permitted. Their first priority was the barn conversion project.

So confident was Jim in his new life that he had contacted a couple of old army mates who had tried to keep in touch but he had previously found it too hard to be reminded of anyone from that time. They had taken it in turns to ring him periodically but Jim had never felt able to see them. However both George "Jono" Johnson and Mike "Windy" Gale had been good mates and he wanted to invite them over from Newcastle. He told Lizzie he now felt the time was right to share his newfound happiness with old friends whose steadfast support over the years clearly demonstrated how deeply they cared about him.

Lizzie was worried he would be upset if he saw people from his past, however these were old comrades who shared a common history, so maybe it would be good for him to meet up with them again. With a degree of trepidation, she agreed to the idea and welcomed them to the pub.

She need not have worried, Jim was delighted to see them and in turn, they were amazed at his progress. They were both typical army types Lizzie thought; quite physically strong and not dissimilar to Jim in appearance, although Windy was a couple of inches shorter. They had both left the army and Windy worked in security for a large retail company. Jono dabbled a bit in various ventures, calling himself an entrepreneur. He had lots of ideas, his latest was to set up a company specialising in adventure type holidays in the area, so Jim's call had come at an opportune time. He could see the potential for using the Blenny as a watering hole for his clients.

Work was due to start on the barn conversion soon and Lizzie was keen to explore the adventure holiday proposition. If Jono's idea worked, they could offer packed lunches and dinners each day for his clients.

Maybe they could sort something out with the local hotel for accommodation. Lizzie loved nothing more than getting her teeth into a new venture; she actually surprised herself as Richard always said she had no head for business. Anyway no time to think of Richard and his doubts about her abilities – just carry on!

And carry on she did. Life was panning out pretty well for Lizzie – what could go wrong? In the small hours of the night though, sometimes shadows from the past encroached into her dreams. What would Richard think if he saw her now – would he be proud of her? What would her life be like if he had not died? As usual, she managed to force her mind away from dark thoughts and look forward to the future and whatever that may hold.

At that time Lizzie had no possible notion of how much she was tempting fate.

Chapter 5

An Unexpected Visitor – 1996

All was well in Lizzie's world.

Wonderfully small issues occupied her mind and a particular bugbear currently, and indeed the talk of Blenthorne and Rowendale for that matter, was the vicar's broken washing machine. Lizzie grinned to herself as she remembered how it had impacted on the life of almost everyone who had had occasion to encounter the vicar over the last couple of weeks.

Every time Lizzie saw him he mentioned his ailing appliance – to the extent she had taken to finding shop windows incredibly interesting and even the windows of people's houses, so that he could not catch her attention in the village. She realised on one occasion she was staring avidly at a china cat in the window of a cottage near to the information centre and public toilets. On another, she had bolted into the post office where it appeared two other villagers had also taken refuge until the vicar had traversed the length of the street, apparently eagerly on the look-out for people with whom to share his woes.

Hilary Cole the postmistress looked towards the window clearly trying to determine what was so enthralling it had mesmerised Lizzie and her companions. It was doubtful that she was any the wiser even after she had observed the collective sigh of relief when the vicar was no longer in sight. As the other two left, Lizzie felt obliged to buy a book of second class stamps to explain her presence. She departed without enlightening Hilary. No doubt the vicar himself would feel the need to venture into the post office to share his troubles with her before long. Indeed Lizzie was surprised he had not done so already!

Lizzie did feel slightly guilty that she was avoiding him as he was a very sincere gentleman, totally committed to his calling. Unfortunately he had lately become obsessed with the issue of getting his clothes laundered and every conversation was steered to this seemingly insurmountable problem. To Lizzie's dismay he somehow managed to weave a reference to it into his sermon the previous Sunday.

Yes, even in a talk about Saul of Tarsus on the Road to Damascus, the intrepid vicar, Reverend Simeon Humphries, "Si-to-my-friends-and-enemies-alike", was heard to remark on the importance of clean clothes. Lizzie was sure she was not the only member of the congregation supressing an incongruous giggle.

Worse still, he had taken to holding audience in the public bar. He seemed to think it appropriate for the inhabitants of Blenthorne and Rowendale to "substantially contribute" to the repair of the washing machine. He argued appropriate vestments were essential to his pastoral life and without the aforementioned appliance, how could the long suffering Gloria his dutiful wife, be expected to keep him in sartorial elegance or words to that effect. He would have no alternative other than to appear in church, in public and indeed in people's homes wearing clothes from jumble sales – looking like a scarecrow. He alas would be reduced to buying such items as he had nothing left in his wardrobe until his machine was in working order again.

Lizzie had had enough at this point – the thought of poor Gloria up to her elbows in soapsuds fighting a losing battle to keep her husband's ecclesiastical apparel pristine was just too much. She was worried that "Si-to-his-friends-and-enemies-alike" would soon start driving away her customers, so she announced she would put a fundraising tin on the bar to see if enough coinage could be mustered to pay for the repair if that would mean he would please stop talking about it. There were a few "hear hears" from the regulars in the bar that night and she thought they probably all hoped that the good reverend might have the godly grace to look a tad embarrassed – but not a bit of it! He sank back happily into his chair clearly satisfied he had got his own way.

She was still smiling to herself when she closed the bar after the last lunchtime customer had left. How she loved the absurd minutiae of life.

She was looking forward to a cup of tea and a bit of mindless afternoon TV. No Alex or Jim to worry about because they were away at camp and thankfully no paying guests in situ. Just as she was about to leave the bar after a final look round to satisfy herself that all was in place for the evening, there was a knock at the door. She would ignore it. The opening times were clearly displayed on a sign outside. However, there was another knock and a woman's voice called out:

'Hello, anyone there?'

Hopefully it wouldn't take long to get rid of her, Lizzie thought optimistically. With that in mind she opened the door slightly. She saw standing before her a woman of about her own height but certainly a lot slimmer and several years younger. She was wearing a dark tailored well-fitting pinstriped trouser suit and crisp white blouse open at the neck. She had a largish white faux leather shoulder bag tucked under her left arm with its strap dangling down. Smart white high heeled court shoes Lizzie noticed – a bit common her mother would have said. Her blonde wavy hair tumbled around her shoulders and her makeup appeared immaculate.

'Yes, can I help you?' Lizzie asked through the small crack in the door.

'I'm looking for Jim Lockwood,' said the woman. 'Are you his employer, I was told he worked and lived here?'

'By whom?' asked Lizzie frostily, ever mindful and protective of Jim.

'Jono, a friend from his army days,' replied the blonde.

'You had better come in then,' Lizzie said as she opened the door sufficiently to admit the stranger. Her hair bounced as she walked Lizzie, noticed enviously.

She would take her into the office and set her straight – Jim had made so much progress, seeing someone from the past could send him back to square one. He had been happy to see Windy and Jono but that was his choice and not a surprise out of the blue. People really should not just turn up from way back and expect a warm welcome, certainly not people that looked like she did.

A horrific thought descended on Lizzie like a heavy weight. Way back – oh my glory, could this possibly be Sarah? She somehow knew it was only a matter of time. She remembered the day of the Dock Tarn walk when Jim had talked openly about Sarah. He would always love her; he had been completely honest about that. Lizzie had a sense of foreboding at the time, a feeling that if Sarah ever reappeared in Jim's life, that would be the end of their relationship and her happiness.

So this was the day where it all started to fall apart, or it would have been if he had been here. She did not want to ask her outright, as that would give the appearance of concern. Stay cool, be nonchalant, thought Lizzie.

'Would you like some coffee?' asked Lizzie as politely as she could.

'Actually, yes please – black with one sugar; I have had a bit of a journey to get here – I have left my car in your car park at the back, there was no one else parked there, that's okay isn't it – the hatchback?' said the unsolicited caller as she gracefully arranged herself on one of the upright chairs set at an angle to the desk. She leaned over and placed her car keys on the desk, dropping her bag down next to her and crossing her long slim legs as she did so.

Lizzie moved into the kitchen.

'Is Jim here?' asked the blonde loudly enough for Lizzie to hear.

'What do you want to see him about?' called Lizzie from the kitchen whilst putting extra sugar in the coffee, at least that should go straight to her hips Lizzie thought with a vague feeling of triumph.

'Um, I'm not sure I can tell you,' said Lizzie's unwanted guest, 'it is sort of ... um well, a private matter, between Jim and I.' So this was Sarah, decided Lizzie with a sadness filling her heart, a private matter indeed between Jim and Sarah, of which of course she had no part.

Lizzie's mind was racing. Why had she come here? Why now? Jim was so settled, he loved her – not quite with the intensity that she loved him but enough for them to be happy and contented together. Her world would be destroyed by this woman waltzing back into his life and wrecking everything they had painstakingly built together. Alex would be devastated; he and Jim had the most wonderful relationship. All this would be torn apart by the reappearance of Jim's ex.

Lizzie had taken pity on the lonely anxious man who had arrived on her doorstep and gradually he had started to enjoy things again. A spark flickered occasionally in his eyes in the beginning and then more regularly as he had started to believe he could lead a fulfilling life, in spite of the unspeakable things he had witnessed and lived through.

She had wrapped him in love and security until he became well in body and mind. What had Sarah done – abandoned him when he needed her the most. Lizzie saw her happy bubble bursting; her life falling around her like leaves from trees in autumn and being blown away on the breeze. Lizzie felt sick as a wave of anxiety swept her body. Her fingers started to tingle as her lungs deprived her hands and feet of oxygen and she felt unsteady.

'Jim and I have no secrets,' she said tersely, her heart pounding as she walked rather slowly, so as not to lose her balance, back into the office. She placed the tray with the coffee and some hopefully very fattening biscuits on the desk to the side of the slim young woman.

The cool confident creature circumvented the calorie crammed chocolate chip cookies.

'Oh currant biscuits, my favourite,' she said in a patronising sort of way. 'Sorry to be vague, but you are his employer aren't you? I certainly wouldn't tell my boss everything – particularly not, um, well, private stuff.'

Lizzie did not reply but felt her body tense all over and her lips purse involuntarily as she waited in silence for the penny to drop.

Her unwelcome companion looked quizzically at Lizzie for a few moments and then said in a rush, 'Oh! Heavens! –

forgive me.' She paused to giggle – not even attempting to keep the disbelief out of her voice as her eyes danced with barely disguised mirth.

'It really didn't occur to me that you might be ... well, um you know, anything more.'

'Why not?' asked Lizzie who was having quite a lot of difficulty keeping her breathing even.

'Well it's just ... um, you don't look, I mean ...' the cruel reply petered out. Again she giggled unkindly but slightly more nervously this time, as she quite blatantly looked Lizzie up and down.

'Why not?' repeated Lizzie trying to keep the anger out of her voice but realising she was not being entirely successful.

She was well aware that she did not look her best at that particular moment having been up since 6:30 a.m. and hardly stopping for as much as a drink since. Even if she had made an effort, she could not compete with the attractive woman in front of her. Her hair was all over the place, she had made countless tuna sandwiches and smoked mackerel salads at lunchtime and she thought she probably smelled of fish. She even had a smear of mayonnaise down her jeans.

'Well, I mean I wouldn't have thought ... um, it's probably best if I go now if Jim isn't here. I will catch up with him later.'

The mocking blonde shook her head as amusement got the better of her again. Lizzie was convinced she smirked.

Yes I am sure you will, thought Lizzie as she contemplated the future. Jim meeting up with his ex again, feeling dreadful and struggling with his conscience because of the feelings he undoubtedly had for Lizzie but in the end, he would go.

She knew this woman sitting so smugly in her office was in a different league. She would turn heads wherever she went. Lizzie couldn't compete with that; she was pleasant looking but "homely".

And there the interloper sat, as bold as brass, belittling Lizzie. A flash of fury shot through Lizzie like a bolt of lightning. She could feel blood pounding in her temples which was making a coursing sound in her ears as her heart thumped wildly and erratically in her chest. She would not allow this. She had not spent over two years nurturing a damaged man back to health just for his ex to reclaim him now that he was well again. She was visibly shaking and struggling to breathe.

'I know who you are and why you have come here,' said Lizzie passionately, her cheeks flushing as she stood squarely in front of the younger woman's chair.

'Do you indeed!' the bold reply came as the composed woman leant back in the chair and placed her left elbow on the arm with her hand to her chin. 'I think that is highly unlikely,' she smiled. 'However you are clearly extremely hot-tempered and more than a little unstable if you really want my opinion. I mean look at you, you are all flushed and panting with rage for no reason whatsoever. Why on earth anyone would want to be with you is beyond me but each to their own choice I suppose.'

'You know nothing of our life together, you can't imagine what he means to me, what we mean to each other,' Lizzie screamed, completely losing any remnants of equanimity.

'No, I probably can't,' came the heartless reply, 'and quite frankly I don't want to. I can see myself out.' She rose from the chair, picked up her bag and turned to reach for her car keys. She laughed again. 'All I can say is poor Jim.'

Actually that was the last thing she ever said.

What happened next took Lizzie completely by surprise. Something seemed to snap inside her head and frenzied wrath spewed out of her like molten lava erupting from a volcano. As her nemesis turned to bend and collect her keys, Lizzie picked up the closest thing to hand, namely a heavy marble paperweight, given to her by her mother-in-law one year as a Christmas present. She had always hated it and had never used it; until now.

Lizzie lunged at the spiteful blonde with all her might. She seemed to possess superhuman strength as she clouted the unsuspecting woman over the head with the heavy object in her hand. Lizzie involuntarily let out a scream. The focus of Lizzie's fury gave a small moan as she tried to turn round, putting her right hand to her head as she did so and attempting to fend off another blow with the other arm and hand. She had a look of shock and bewilderment on her face as she cowered away from the blows raining down on her. Lizzie hit her again and again with the paperweight and eventually she fell back into the chair.

When the shock of the moment had passed, Lizzie saw what she had done. She was breathing very fast, shaking and shivering as she looked at the sticky mess on the surface of the paperweight with bits of matted slime slowly dripping to the floor. She looked towards the chair and saw that the still figure had slumped to the left side at a very uncomfortable looking angle with a dark stain streaking down her long blonde hair. Maybe she could say it had been an accident. Yes that might work; she had tripped and fallen into her uninvited visitor with the paperweight in her outstretched hand as she tried to stop herself from falling.

She walked round to stand in front of the inert form. She was very pale and Lizzie placed both hands on the motionless woman's arms and shook her slightly.

'Sarah – you are Sarah aren't you? Are you okay, I'm sorry I must have tripped and hit you accidentally,' she said lamely.

No response, she seemed to be out cold. With shaking hands, Lizzie felt for the pulse in the younger woman's carotid artery. It was faint and as Lizzie continued to press her finger to the slim neck, it faltered and faded completely. Lizzie walked to the window and stared at the world outside with unseeing eyes. This could not have happened, it was a very bad dream – in fact she had had one the other night involving Richard and upon waking, everything was fine. When she turned around, there would be no one there at all. It happened like that sometimes in dreams. However, she would not look just yet, she would pop upstairs first and make a hot drink.

*

Lizzie left the office and locked the door putting the key in her pocket. She went upstairs and put the TV on. Goodness what a mess all over her hands. She washed them quickly, twice. A quiz programme to watch, she quite liked those. She absentmindedly glanced at the TV for a while, pacing up and down. She went downstairs again and unlocked the door to the office.

It hadn't been a dream, the body was still there; half slumped in the chair and half on the floor. She picked up the phone to call the police. She dialled the first two nines and then calmly replaced the receiver. Thinking it through, no one had asked this interloper to come here. No one had asked her to look down her nose and pass judgement on Lizzie's relationship with Jim. No one had asked her to laugh in Lizzie's face. More to the point, no one had seen her since she had arrived, the pub was empty. The car park was empty too and there had been no one outside when Lizzie had let her in.

An idea started to form in Lizzie's mind. Maybe, just maybe she could make this go away. A plan quickly formulated in her mind. She could make it look like a walking accident. She went upstairs and rummaged in her wardrobe. Yes, there were the walking trousers she was keeping until she lost two stone and fitted into them again. They would do perfectly. Her spare walking boots were there also. Lizzie found a top and some socks. She added her old cagoule as no one in their right minds walks in the Lake District without some form of outer clothing, even in the summer.

She went quickly back to the office. She had an hour and a half before Maggie arrived to start her evening shift behind the bar. Bodies did not bother her. Her nursing training meant she had handled more than she could remember. She locked the office door behind her. She turned competently to the task in hand. The body was getting cold but still pliable and Lizzie laid it on the floor and removed the outer clothing and shoes. With a degree of difficulty and quite a bit of cursing, she finally managed to dress the body in the clothes she had brought from her bedroom. She checked the pockets were empty.

She could not afford any oversights such as something in a pocket which could tie any of the garments to Lizzie. She pushed on the walking boots which thankfully were more or less the correct size. She tied the matted blonde hair back in a band as obviously people would not walk with hair flowing everywhere, at least not if they were serious about it. She then placed a plastic bag over the head to prevent transference of bodily fluids onto any more surfaces in the office. The head was a bit of a mess if Lizzie was honest but she felt sure falls from a great height onto rock could cause such damage.

She bundled the dead woman's shoulder bag, clothes and shoes into a large plastic bag which had been used to cover the new tumble dryer when it had been delivered. Jim said there was a dent in the front, she would look at that later and see if she needed to ring the shop. However, they might want their bag back if they were going to replace the appliance. Lizzie removed the things and found several supermarket carrier bags, divided the offending articles into these and shoved them in the bottom drawer of the desk, having removed the original contents first. She would deal with those tomorrow. She locked the drawer and put the key in her pocket. Thinking about it, she went back to the drawer and unlocking it, removed the shoes, as they might not be easy to dispose of. Lizzie then locked the drawer again.

She checked outside was clear; often walkers wandered into the car park even when the pub was shut. Jim and Alex had gone off for their expedition by minibus, leaving their large estate at home. Lizzie then went out to bring the car as close to the back door as possible. After moving the vehicle, she picked up the old piece of carpet from the utility room floor which was covering the broken tiles. Her grandmother would have laughed at the description "utility room"; she would have called it "the scullery". What a bizarre thing to remember at that particular moment Lizzie thought as she walked back to the office.

She found some string in the top drawer of the desk and cut several lengths with the scissors which were also kept there. She stretched the carpet out on the floor and rolled the body into it. Lizzie tied up the bundle as best she could with the string. Checking the coast was still clear she dragged the carpet with its gruesome contents to the back door and with great difficulty heaved and pushed it into the back of the car. Her heart was pounding as she did so. She went to the barn and found the wheelbarrow. She placed this in the back of the car also and having spread the car rug over the top, moved it back to its normal parking spot.

Lizzie went back to the office, found the keys to the hatchback and picked up the shoes – nearly new she thought and nice quality. She went outside and unlocked the car. Having placed the shoes in the boot, she drove it into the barn and closed the door.

Lizzie went back to the office. Surprisingly not too much mess to clear up; the odd fleck of debris on the walls but she was planning to decorate anyway. Her watch told her she had a few minutes left. She cleaned the back of the chair and the spots on the walls with liquid detergent and used carpet cleaner and then a bit of bleach on the short pile carpet. Thankfully the colour did not run. She realised that would have to do for now and opening the door, quickly ran upstairs to shower and change before Maggie arrived and the customers started turning up.

'Nice afternoon?' said Maggie cheerfully as she arrived.

'Bit boring actually,' said Lizzie hoping her voice sounded normal.

'Well make the most of it because the boys will be back on Friday with loads of washing no doubt. In fact the forecast for tomorrow is foul, so I wouldn't be surprised if their camping trip was cut short and they came home early! Oh, Lizzie, are you okay you have cut your finger. Come on let's get it under some cold water.'

'No I'm fine don't worry, the glass just slipped out of my hand,'

Maggie was leading Lizzie through to the kitchen.

'Oh, have you been cleaning?' she said looking round and sniffing the air in an exaggerated manner.

'Yes it really is my day for dropping things. Bottle of wine all over the carpet in the office! I was just wondering about getting some more of that red we got on special offer from the supplier, it seems popular at the moment, walked through to the office with the bottle in my hand and next thing I knew, all over the floor.'

The finger was washed and plastered to Maggie's satisfaction and she went back through the bar as it was time to open the door.

'Alright, alright I'm coming,' she called in answer to the loud banging.

Lizzie looked round the office again. Something was niggling. Had she missed something? No all looked to be in order and no sign of the events of earlier in the day – almost as if nothing had happened at all.

*

Lizzie got through the evening in a trance. Nothing seemed real and she was really grateful when it was time to close up for the night. She saw Maggie off and turned in herself for a few hours. She set her alarm for 4:00 a.m. but only dozed fitfully and was already up, bathed and dressed before the alarm went off. She left the building and set off in the estate. She realised her audacious plan would only work if there was no one else around.

The day was dull and overcast with mist and drizzle in the air. For once she was very grateful for that. Lizzie had spent the night thinking of the best place in which to dispose of a body and decided on Hell's Drop about five miles from home. The east side of the peak was easily accessible for an experienced walker but to the west the terrain was much less hospitable. There were gullies and crags which looked spectacular but were virtually impenetrable and only the extremely foolhardy would attempt an assent from that side.

Lizzie drove the car up the narrow road leading to the start of the climb, to the point where she could take it no further. She parked in a layby and got the wheelbarrow out of the back and with an enormous struggle got the rolled carpet into a transportable position over it.

Somehow she managed to push the wheelbarrow over the stony ground, stumbling every few yards, with the wind and drizzle slapping her in the face with every step and stray bits of wet hair dripping in her eyes. When it was impractical to push the wheelbarrow any further Lizzie removed her hideous bundle, falling over again in the process. She then dragged the carpet for as long as she could and with her physical strength almost gone she decided this spot would have to do. She unfurled the carpet, took off the bag covering the head and rolled the body away from the rough path to the edge of the drop. At least she hoped it was the edge, she knew this area well but with the mist and drizzle which was turning to rain – it was difficult to be completely sure of her bearings. She stuffed the bag into her coat pocket.

Lizzie then sat on the ground just behind the body and with what was left of her depleted strength, thrust her feet forward to make contact with the torso and in a sudden rush it rolled out of sight. Lizzie had no way of knowing if it had fallen a few feet, or the hundred or so feet she hoped. She could hear nothing. There was no more she could do; she just had to hope that when the remains were discovered the damage to the body looked consistent with injuries sustained in a fall.

Lizzie retraced her steps which was not as easy as it sounded as the mist was now so thick she could barely see five feet in front of her. She regained the rough path and found the carpet which she rolled up and retied with the string. It was quite heavy on its own and awkward to carry as it was now completely sodden. She made her way back to where she hoped to also be reunited with the wheelbarrow, carrying the heavy water-soaked carpet under her arm as best she could. The rain could now be defined as relentless and torrential as it pelted Lizzie from all angles. Her feet were soaked and squelched in her boots as she stumbled along.

When she found the wheelbarrow Lizzie placed the carpet on top and wheeled it as fast as she could to the estate. Once there she loaded up and climbed into the driver's seat, she was soaked to the skin. She turned the car round and drove home as quickly as the conditions would allow, not quite believing what she had done. However there was no time for complacency; she still had the car and personal possessions to dispose of.

Lizzie wondered how long it would be before Sarah was reported missing. Jim had told her that she was an only child but with a sudden pang of conscience Lizzie thought about Sarah's parents. She pushed the thought from her mind as quickly as she could.

Sarah had been the architect of her own destiny the minute she had decided to try to wreck Lizzie's life.

Lizzie got back to the pub and went inside. She had a bath and put her clothes into the washing machine. She put some powder into the plastic ball and shoved it in, setting the programme to "heavy soil" as she did so. She then stuffed her walking boots with newspaper to aid the drying process before leaving them by the back door,

She remembered the bag in the pocket of her coat and took it out. She stashed it in the drawer of the desk with the dead woman's things along with the string she had used to tie her bundle. The sodden carpet roll she left in the barn to dispose of later.

The office looked tidy. Lizzie decided to leave the personal items until she could have a bonfire. Not practical on a day like today. She had a piece of toast and left a note for Maggie to say she had gone into Carlisle as she had heard that there was a sale on at the fabric shop she liked and she was going to order some curtains for the bedrooms in the flat. She thought she should have been exhausted by her exertions but no doubt adrenaline was driving her on.

Lizzie collected the hatchback from the barn. She then drove to the closest bus stop which was in Rowendale about two miles from Blenthorne. She left the car a short distance from the stop. It was now about 10:00 a.m. and the bus was due at ten minutes past the hour. When it arrived she got on and bought a return ticket to Carlisle, just in case she needed to use this as an alibi later. She had seen a film where a similar alibi was used, only to find the bus was cancelled – or had it been a theatre performance that was cancelled? Anyway, she would not be making that mistake.

Lizzie still could not shake the idea that she had missed something in the office. She got off at the first stop after Rowendale, hopefully unnoticed as several people were getting on. She hurried back to the car as quickly as possible, running and stumbling a bit as she did so. She drove uneventfully to Carlisle and left the hatchback in one of the larger car parks with the doors unlocked and the keys in the ignition.

She then went to her favourite fabric shop and chose the material for her curtains. She gave the measurements to the assistant who said she would give Lizzie a call when the curtains were ready. At least now she had her story straight for her presence in Carlisle if needed.

She caught the bus back to Rowendale and as she was contemplating the walk back to the pub, began to relax. All was going well so far. Then she heard a familiar voice.

'Hello Lizzie, on foot?' It was Dave, a mechanic from the local garage.

'Yes, blooming car wouldn't start this morning.'

'Let me give you a lift, I am going into Blenthorne – where have you been?'

'Thank you; that would be great.'

Hell and damnation. Thinking quickly on her feet, Lizzie told him about her trip to Carlisle and the fabric shop sale that was ending the following day. She calculated – correctly – that Dave would not be even remotely interested in her curtains and would switch off as she prattled on.

He dropped her at the pub and asked if she would like him to have a look at the car and she said it was probably the plugs and being the daughter of a mechanic, she could manage that herself. However, if not, she would ring him later or maybe even leave it for Jim and he could take it to the specialist garage in Keswick.

She told him to drop in and she would buy him a drink sometime. They said their goodbyes and Lizzie walked thankfully into the pub. Maggie was behind the bar and said it had been fairly quiet as the weather was clearly putting folk off their hiking and drinking.

Maggie was still talking and suddenly Lizzie was listening with intent.

'... so I had a few minutes this morning and I washed it thoroughly – goodness knows what was on it, all thick and sticky and it looked like hair or something attached.'

'What looked like it had hair attached?' asked Lizzie sharply, holding her breath.

'The paperweight in the office; as I just said, I went in to get the phone number for the supplier as the Ladies loo thingy dispenser is playing up again.'

'Oh, well I had been using it as a door stop,' said Lizzie trying to sound casual.

Maggie looked surprised.

'Sorry; the tampon dispenser from the Ladies? Why would you use that as a door stop?'

'No Maggie, the paperweight. I think it probably got caught up in the incident with the red wine. However, it has been on the floor for a while so frankly it could be anything.'

So that is what was niggling away at her; the paperweight! She had left it in the office. Well that was that, she would never get away with it now; first Dave and the lift home and now Maggie and the ruddy paperweight, not to mention the tampon dispenser.

She got through the remainder of the day without further incident.

The next day dawned just as bright as the previous day had been miserable. Jim and Alex had not arrived back so their trip was obviously continuing, for which Lizzie was very grateful. She needed an early start to get her bonfire going. She took the contents from the bottom drawer of the desk and went outside to set about finding some kindling to get the fire started. Would it all burn? Would the bag burn? She had no way of knowing.

She resisted the temptation to empty the bag's contents as seeing her rival's personal possessions would have been too much. All were deposited along with some rubbish that had been accumulating in the barn for months and the fire was started in the usual spot, behind the small rockery that Lizzie had created. The carpet was still too wet to burn so she left it at the back of the barn and would say there had been an accident with the washing machine.

'Hope that isn't Jim's clothes you're burning there Lizzie,' called Naomi, Jim's former landlady.

'No, not this time! You're up early Naomi,' said Lizzie seeing the elderly lady limping along the road in front of the pub.

'Well it's Seth. He is really poorly so I was just going to go to the phone box to ring the vet again.' Naomi had no phone at her cottage.

'Sorry to hear that, you and Seth have been together a long time.' Lizzie had quite a soft spot for Naomi's old collie.

'By the way, did I see you driving a different car yesterday morning – a smallish one?' asked Naomi conversationally as she walked slowly towards Lizzie.

'Um no, why would you think that?' asked Lizzie hoping her voice sounded even and clear as she stoked her fire.

'I could have sworn it was you, it looked like you – I rang the vet yesterday as well you see and he said to call back today if Seth was no better and on my way back from the phone box, I saw you in a different car, it was a sort of yellow colour.'

'I had trouble with the estate and I got the bus in Rowendale as I needed to go to Carlisle, so it certainly wasn't me. Wish it had been, it would have saved me from getting soaked,' said Lizzie cheerfully, her heart beating so loud she was surprised Naomi could not hear it.

'I do hope Seth is okay Naomi. See you soon, bye.'

Lizzie turned and walked back to the door. Once inside she closed it firmly and stood there shaking for a few moments. She finally got a grip of herself and then went upstairs and had a bath before starting the rituals of the day. After the lunchtime rush she cleared out the study and set to work putting a coat of emulsion on the ceiling and walls after washing them thoroughly.

She checked on the bonfire periodically and was pleased to see that it had taken well and by the end of the day all that remained were ashes. She piled a bit more rubbish onto the site just to make sure everything was disposed of completely. She would find an excuse to have another bonfire at the weekend.

Jim and Alex returned from their camping expedition on the Friday – happy, damp, tired, filthy and full of stories which Lizzie barely heard but she clearly made the appropriate responses, as they didn't appear to notice she was distracted.

She didn't need to use the excuse of the washing machine as Jim didn't even see that the carpet was missing. He did compliment her on painting the office though, suggesting that he and Alex should go away more regularly if that was what she got up to when they were not there!

Lizzie shivered involuntarily.

*

Lizzie waited for the body to be found but nothing happened as day followed day and week followed week. Life seemed to return to normal, at least on the surface. No one appeared to notice that Lizzie jumped every time the phone rang and looked over her shoulder on each occasion that anyone with whom she was unfamiliar addressed her by name.

Amazingly the locals coughed up enough money for Reverend Si's washing machine to be repaired. Not without a little friendly persuasion from Maggie who took to jangling the tin stationed on the bar at everyone who came in. The consequence of not contributing she explained would be more of the same lamenting from the good reverend and they could all do without that.

In fact unbridled joy prevailed in Blenthorne on the day the machine was restored to full working order as the Reverend's smalls (which in fact were anything but) were again to be seen flying majestically like flags from Gloria's saintly washing line in the vicarage garden. Rev Si could once again minister to his flock, resplendent in priestly attire. A sigh of relief was breathed by all and it was hoped fervently that no other appliances failed in the vicarage in the near future. Somehow Lizzie's reaction was a little muted.

Lizzie had the office re-carpeted and bought new chairs. She had the tiles replaced in the utility room. Once the roll of carpet was dry enough she had planned to burn it, but fortuitously noticed a skip on the outskirts of the village at the home belonging to one of the mums from school. She and her husband were having some work done on their cottage and she readily agreed that Lizzie could drop off her old carpet. So that was another link with the incident dealt with.

She waited. The weeks turned into months. Nothing happened. No body. No police investigation. No reports of a missing person.

Lizzie wondered if after all it really had just been a bad dream.

Chapter 6

Developments and Surprises – 1997/9

To anyone that knew her, it would seem that Lizzie Tennyson's life continued as normal over the coming months.

She had come to trust Jim totally and rarely made a decision without consulting him first. He had long since stopped taking a salary and they had even set up a joint bank account, although the Blenthorne Inn was still in Lizzie's name.

After the "incident" as she had taken to thinking of it, she decided there was no point in waiting for the worst to happen, she had to enjoy life as it presented itself. To that end she threw herself into as many community activities as possible – time and pub permitting. The village hall was greatly in need of repair and refurbishment and she suggested to the local council that any profits made by the amateur dramatic society should be channelled into doing it up as there were insufficient funds in the municipal coffers.

The Blenthorne Brigade had put together a few productions in recent times; among them a comedy. Well actually it was more of a farce but that was unintentional, a straight drama, which was a little over ambitious and also slightly farcical, and another pantomime. In this production the leading lady was supposed to be woken by a charming prince – sadly so late was the prince arriving on stage, the aforementioned lady had actually nodded off. She awoke with a start and uttered a string of expletives before she realised where she was – oh well, all part of life's rich tapestry.

With lots of friendly persuasion and indeed a little bullying, Lizzie found that several local businesses were prepared to make a substantial contribution towards the cost of the pantomime production in return for advertising space on posters and in the programmes, the latter of which were readily available to purchase at the Blenthorne Inn and other establishments in the village.

Lizzie and Maggie between them even managed to persuade visitors to the area to buy programmes and give small donations even though they would be far away at the time of the performances.

'You see, it is only with generous giving by people such as yourselves that enables places like Blenthorne to thrive – so many people would move away and the village would die if we could not generate enough income to keep the locals here. Village life flourishes when communities get together to do things like this ...' Maggie was overheard to say to one group of walkers as she collected their empty glasses and relieved them of their money.

The annual village fete was proving to be a very good money spinner with all proceeds going to a variety of local charitable causes. Lizzie always gave a couple of barrels of beer for the refreshment tent and also provided the evening barbecue free of charge so that all proceeds were ploughed into the community. Tourists loved to see the friendly village rivalries, played to the hilt by willing participants, in the jam making and cake competitions, the archery and not forgetting the wet sponge throwing. Along with this came the carnival procession and the fireworks on the village green at the end of the evening.

As proceedings were drawing to a close at the end of another successful event, Jim linked his arm through Lizzie's as they watched the bonfire crackle and hiss.

'Life is pretty good isn't it?' he said with a smile.

Lizzie felt the warmth of the fire on her face and Jim standing close to her.

'Perfect,' she said softly. In fact she could not imagine being happier than she was at that moment.

*

Lizzie was very pleased with the conversion of the barn. They had kept the exposed beams and even the walls had the rough wattle and daub finish associated with barns of the period, all skilfully recreated by the contractor. The floor was a light polished wood with a special non-slip finish. The end nearest to the pub was fitted out as a kitchen with its own entrance and a storage floor above. The restaurant could take up to thirty covers and each table was only booked once per evening; the idea was to give diners the opportunity to enjoy a gastronomic experience in an atmosphere that was calm and tranquil. Lizzie liked the idea of crisp white tablecloths and napkins to match, despite the laundry bill. What price elegance she argued.

The restaurant was proving a great success; they had still to decide on a proper name and currently called it the Blenthorne Inn Restaurant, but that didn't really have much of a ring to it.

Carl was happily installed as head chef with an assistant, kitchen and waiting staff. He and Jim took care of all the hiring for this as Jim had put his savings into the venture. Lizzie was delighted that he had wanted to become so involved and it was good for him to have something of his own.

They decided to offer a quality menu with never more than four main courses from which to choose. As Carl said, anything more and it would be just like any other bistro or fast food diner, taking food straight from the freezer and plonking it in the microwave. They were aiming for elegant fine dining and were pleased to note that the restaurant had already received a very favourable review in the local press.

Windy Gale and Jono's business idea for activity holidays had been given an unexpected boost when the owners of the Fell View Hotel, Robin Corey and Mark Stevens had told Lizzie that they needed to do something about business as a large hotel chain had just purchased the failing Long Lawn Hotel in nearby Rowendale.

'We cannot compete with their prices; we are up to our ears with the bank already,' bemoaned Robin. 'We don't think we can carry on – don't suppose you want to buy a hotel do you Lizzie?'

'No thank you, but I do think it would be a shame if you sold up; we need people like you here. I'm not sure exactly what I can do to help but let me have a think,' said Lizzie.

Lizzie gave the matter due consideration and then spoke to Jim about a possible cash injection from themselves with the proviso that Fell View came in on the activity holiday venture. He weighed up the pros and cons and decided it was a sound proposition and contacted Jono and Windy.

After a meeting with the interested parties it was decided Jono and Windy would organise the holidays and host the groups as well as doing the marketing, and Lizzie and Jim in conjunction with Robin and Mark would organise accommodation via Fell View with the option of eating the evening meal at the restaurant or at the hotel.

The evening after they had signed the paperwork for the activities holidays, Lizzie and Jim were just settling down with a cup of coffee after closing time; Lizzie found herself dropping off to sleep on the sofa when she heard Jim's voice in the distance. She roused herself as she thought he had asked her a question.

'Sorry Jim, what did you say?'

'I was just asking you if a chap called Tony had been in touch; Jono asked me about it yesterday – has he rung at all?'

'No not that I know of, Maggie would have mentioned it if she had taken a call I'm sure. Why, who is he?'

'He sells life insurance and Jono was going to put him in touch with me but that was months ago and I haven't heard anything further, never mind – it's his loss.'

'Why do you need life insurance all of a sudden?' asked Lizzie.

'Well with commitment comes responsibility, so I thought I had better get things in order before getting married. Anyway if he does ring, I have sorted it with the bank now so he has missed his chance.'

'Who are you marrying if you don't mind me asking? Anyone I know?' asked Lizzie trying to sound nonchalant.

'Well I thought I might marry you if you haven't got any better offers in the pipeline.'

Lizzie could hardly believe her ears. She tried to sound casual.

'Um well, not that I can think of at the moment anyway.' She hoped Jim didn't notice from her demeanour that her heart was fit to burst with joy.

Jim never overstated his feelings. Other than the day of the Dock Tarn walk, he barely spoke of how he felt, so Lizzie was not surprised the proposal had been a bit low key, but all that mattered was that he cared for her sufficiently to want to marry her.

About ten weeks later with a minimum of fuss or drama, Lizzie Tennyson became Lizzie Lockwood in a register office ceremony in Keswick, with a reception at Fell View courtesy of Robin and Mark. Their friends from the village came for the reception and Lizzie's parents came up from Bournemouth. Apparently there was a rumour that her mother had smiled on one occasion however this could not be substantiated and the report remained unconfirmed. She certainly found several opportunities to sniff.

'Oh Lizzie – do you really think that dress suits you – isn't it a little showy?' she said pulling a face that only she could manage.

'Mum please, just for one day can you be positive. You haven't seen your grandson for ages, how about you spend some time with him and stop worrying about what I'm wearing. And for your information yes, I do think the dress is appropriate for the occasion otherwise I wouldn't be getting married in it.'

'I suppose this means you won't be coming to live at home with us then,' said her mother somewhat rhetorically, managing a large sniff as she lapsed into silence.

'I was never coming to live with you. Bournemouth is lovely but it isn't my home, you and dad moved there when you retired. This is where I belong, these are my friends and family, please understand that.'

They remained for a couple of days and as was becoming a habit with any visit from her parents, Lizzie's father was given the task of placating his wife with regard to each perceived injustice she suffered during her stay. Everyone breathed a sigh of relief when it was time for them to leave.

Richard's parents had sent good wishes from Spain but did not attend, which was a sensible and pragmatic decision Lizzie felt and she was grateful to them for that. Being unable to choose between Jono and Windy as best man, Jim had asked Alex if he would perform the honours and although still a teenager, he was delighted to be asked and accepted readily. Maggie of course was matron of honour.

A few days after their marriage Lizzie had a brainwave.

'I have just thought of the ideal name for the restaurant,' she said triumphantly.

Jim looked at her enquiringly, getting up from their newly acquired computer.

'Lockwood's, obviously!' said Lizzie. 'You have a stake in it anyway and it's now the family name, so what else should it be called?'

Carl was consulted, gave his approval instantly and the rebranding was commenced forthwith.

*

The following spring a bizarre thing happened; something which totally knocked Lizzie for six. Jim had a call from his sister Sheila in County Durham. She was celebrating a "big birthday" soon and planned to have a party. Jim called Lizzie into their sitting room when they were both on a break.

'Lizzie I need to ask you something. Please say if you mind and we won't go, but the thing is, Sheila is having a party for her birthday and she has invited us.'

'Sounds good,' interrupted Lizzie. 'When is it and why should I prefer not to go?'

'Not for a month or so,' said Jim 'but that is not really the issue. The thing is, she said she has already invited Sarah and her husband Ashley Duncan – Sarah my ex that is.'

'Sarah and her husband ... but how ... I mean is she ... I mean .... does she have a husband?' stammered Lizzie.

'Yes I believe he's doing quite well for himself, some sort of property developer and the way house prices shot up a few years ago he's made a mint, well he's not quite a multi-millionaire I don't think, but he has made enough for a very nice lifestyle. They have a huge house in north-west London apparently. The thing is, if you are not comfortable with seeing them, well we can always say we can't get away from the pub, Sheila will understand.'

'So um .... when um ... exactly did Sheila last hear from Sarah?' asked Lizzie with her back to Jim.

'What? I've no idea – I knew they were in touch, they always got on well, but as to how often they see each other, I don't know. Sheila and I don't chat that regularly and when we do, I think she is far too diplomatic to mention Sarah, not that I would mind of course, all in the past obviously,' said Jim, perhaps a little too casually Lizzie thought.

Lizzie started to feel very sick.

*

Lizzie's mind had been in a state of turmoil ever since they received the party invitation. She was counting down the days and found herself constantly thinking about Sarah, who was clearly not dead.

She took ages getting ready for the party and did wonder about saying she was poorly, but that would be a cowardly way out – besides she was never ill, it would be an amazing coincidence if suddenly she had been struck down on the very day she had to meet her husband's ex-wife. What if Jim decided to go alone? No, she had to be there to support him. She wondered what Sarah would be like and how Jim would feel about seeing her again.

More to the point, who was lying at the bottom of Hell's Drop if Sarah was alive and well and happily married to a wealthy property developer? The enormity of what she had done hit her like a steam roller. She had killed someone thinking it was Sarah. She began to shake as she thought of it. Thankfully Jim didn't seem to notice, presumably he too was thinking about the evening ahead, although clearly for different reasons.

They arrived at Sheila and Steve's house fairly early on in the evening. It was a smart detached property in a pleasant village just a few miles to the west of Darlington. Sheila worked at a department store in Darlington as a personal shopper and Steve was a dispensing optician in the town.

They had two daughters both of whom lived close by, the elder girl Phoebe was married and the younger one, Beth shared a flat with a friend. Both were at their parents' house to greet guests as they arrived. Lizzie had met them all before; they were a lovely family and clearly delighted that Jim was happily settled. The girls made a fuss of them as soon as they stepped through the door.

Sheila had taken Lizzie aside on the first occasion they had met over a year ago and told her how pleased they were that Jim had found happiness and contentment in his life and how worried she had previously been about him.

She was on hand now to welcome Lizzie and Jim and hugged them both. As Jim moved across to shake Steve's hand, Sheila linked her arm through Lizzie's and steered her towards the drinks.

'I hope you are both okay about me inviting Sarah and Ashley, I didn't stop to think until it was too late about how it might affect Jim, seeing her again.'

'He is quite happy to do so I think,' said Lizzie a bit nervously. Little did Sheila know it was her that was dreading the next few hours!

Everyone agreed that the evening passed off smoothly. They had invited roughly thirty guests and so it was easy to mingle and move from person to person after a few minutes of polite conversation.

Lizzie had seen Sarah and Ashley Duncan arrive. He was tall and distinguished looking with greying hair. She was elegant and stunningly attractive. Lizzie suddenly felt very dowdy in her sensible black dress. She found herself standing a bit straighter to emphasise her height and bust. She also held her breath to make her stomach look a bit flatter.

She was seemingly engrossed and fascinated by what her current companion was telling her, giving him all her attention, nodding and smiling at him encouragingly. She made a point of not catching Sheila's eye for the inevitable introductions to the newly arrived couple.

Should the need arise, Lizzie had loads to talk about; the pub, the restaurant being ably run by Maggie's husband Carl who had agreed to abandon the oil rigs in favour of life in Blenthorne; oh yes, she could prattle on for hours. Also there was the diversification into adventure holidays and that was before her community commitments, so she didn't have to struggle for something to say if the conversation lagged.

Some minutes later she was listening to a friend of Steve who was explaining the intricacies of wine-making when over his shoulder she saw Sarah and Jim gravitate towards each other.

No don't smile at her, she thought as she nodded politely to the wine-maker with a fixed smile on her face. Don't look at her like that. Don't touch her – don't touch him – don't touch each other. Damn it!

*

Jim was a bit nervous when he saw Sarah approaching and decided to put his glass down so he didn't spill the contents.

'Jim, it really is wonderful to see you, you look well,' said Sarah as she kissed him on both cheeks.

She looked sensational he thought. He remembered the familiar scent of her perfume. She didn't appear to have aged or put on any weight and she was wearing a long tightfitting dress made of something sparkly, he had no idea what, but it looked wonderful on her. Clearly she could now afford to look the part of a property developer's wife; however her greeting to him seemed warm and sincere.

'Hello Sarah.' Jim paused then feeling he needed to add something said, 'you look amazing. I'm glad you came. And Ashley too of course, where is he?' more out of politeness than because he wanted to know.

'Oh boring someone with his future development plans and looking for investors I expect!' said Sarah with a sigh as she smiled at Jim with what he thought might be a tear in her eye. He felt a bit weak at the knees.

They chatted for a few minutes and even to a casual onlooker it must have been apparent that they slipped effortlessly into an easy rapport. Sarah's eyes were sparkling as she laughed at an off-the-cuff remark from Jim. For his part, Jim looked happy and relaxed as they stood closely together.

'Sarah I must find Lizzie and introduce you. She is a very special lady and I am so grateful to her for everything she has done for me.'

'Is gratitude enough to build a life on Jim?' asked Sarah softly. Jim didn't seem to hear her.

'She is just over there and hasn't even noticed I'm talking to you,' he said as he looked round and pointed in Lizzie's direction.

'Bless your heart, she has been aware of us from the very moment we first spoke and hasn't taken her eyes off you since,' said Sarah quietly with a small ironic smile.

Lizzie gritted her teeth for possibly the most difficult encounter of her life but she hoped she pulled it off with grace and dignity. She made polite conversation with Sarah for a few moments and extracted herself as quickly as she could, making sure she had Jim firmly by the arm as she steered him towards the food.

Jim seemed quiet on the way home, tired hopefully rather than upset to have seen Sarah again, or even worse, sad that it was Lizzie he was going home with. They chatted briefly and he fell asleep, allowing her to drive home with her brain in overdrive. As they were leaving Sarah smiled at her and kissed her on the cheek.

'Look after Jim,' she said in a whisper. 'He means the world to me.' Lizzie nodded not trusting herself to speak. Oh my goodness after all she had done and now she could well lose him anyway.

*

As it turned out, she didn't lose him.

Lizzie noticed with interest that Ashley Duncan's name and praise for his business acumen was becoming a regular feature in the press. Lizzie wondered if Jim ever saw the articles. If he did, he never mentioned it.

They had successfully negotiated another Christmas at Blenthorne; the most recent pantomime, had passed off seemingly disaster free, apart from the beanstalk, which Lizzie knew was a bad idea. It had fallen down midway through the second act on the first night but thankfully everyone had taken it in good part and pretended they didn't notice.

The restaurant was fully booked most of the time with good reviews continuing to appear in the press. Jono and Windy's business was going from strength to strength and they were expanding to incorporate more extreme sports. Lizzie was worried it would reduce the profit margins as they would have to pay a huge insurance premium but Jono assured her this would be offset by the amount of money people were prepared to pay to be scared out of their wits.

For clientele who wanted a day off from the thrills of adventure, Carl had been persuaded to offer day courses in pasta making, with participants being allowed to help prepare a pasta course for dinner in the restaurant, if their work passed muster. Should this be the case they were awarded a certificate at the end of the evening. This was also proving popular.

There were continuing clamours for Jim to give evening demonstrations of his balloon animal making skills but so far he had resisted all requests; pointing out they were offering quality holiday experiences, not second rate end-of-the-pier shows. What next – Maggie popping out of a cake maybe? Lizzie did agree that he had a point, though Maggie didn't seem too unhappy at the prospect!

Windy and Jono had started the business by advertising walking and cycling holidays in and around the fells with each holiday tailor-made to suit the requirements of the clients. In addition to this, they branched out into winter adventures when the snow covered the peaks and in better weather, overnight camping trips on the fells, as well as photographic wildlife holidays.

As the business grew they were able to advertise their ability to accommodate just about any type of holiday anyone wanted to book. If they did not have the expertise themselves, they found it through ex-army contacts and sometimes people actually got in touch with them to ask if they would like a specific course run for holidaymakers.

Computers were now commonplace and setting up a website was not too much of an obstacle for Jono who, in true entrepreneurial style, knew exactly the right people to approach for the creation of a suitably professional-looking package. This innovation proved to be a great asset to the business and Jono monitored their "hits" with delight each day. They were getting more queries than they could handle at times and the hotel and restaurant were benefitting enormously.

They had just completed a painting and pottery course, about which they knew little. However, the husband and wife team who supplied the expertise were pleased with the money they made during their week at Blenthorne and said they would be happy to return whenever they were wanted.

In addition, they had recently started gorge walking experiences which involved leaping plunge pools, traversing along rock walls and jumping across boulders. Also it incorporated climbing waterfalls, exploring caves and swinging over torrents. Lizzie thought it sounded terrifying and hoped there would not be any accidents as it was possibly a bit too dangerous for comfort.

Early one evening in late summer, some of the gorge walking participants came into the Blenny lounge bar and ordered drinks. Lizzie smiled at them pleasantly.

'Where did you go today?' she asked conversationally.

'It was amazing,' said a young city type. 'We were at a place called Hell's Drop, almost inaccessible but we got quite a way up into the gorge'.

Lizzie felt a bit sick. She passed over the drinks and taking the money, excused herself, asking Bert to pop through from the other bar to take over.

Three weeks later, on the next gorge walking expedition, the remains of a body were found.

Chapter 7

Discovery – 1999

Alex took the call that changed everything.

'Jim, can you come to the phone? Jono wants to talk to you, says it's urgent.'

'Coming,' called Jim. 'Did he say what he wanted?'

'No, just that it was urgent and that he needed to speak to you,' replied Alex as he put the receiver down and turned to go upstairs.

Jim walked through to the office and picked up the receiver. He talked to Jono for a few minutes, although mostly he just listened.

When Jim put the phone down he came out of the office and went into the bar where Lizzie was chatting and laughing with one of the locals. He suggested that they go upstairs for a chat. He looked concerned as he started up the staircase.

'What's wrong?' Lizzie asked quizzically as they reached the top of the stairs. They entered their flat and Jim made towards the sofa, shutting the door behind them.

'Well, it's the most peculiar thing – you remember the remains they found up near Hell's Drop a few weeks ago? They've identified the body from dental records. She was called Antonia Mason and she was an independent financial adviser. You won't believe this – she was the friend Jono had suggested I speak to regarding the life insurance I took out before we were married.' Jim looked pale as he sat down heavily.

Lizzie stared at him as if mesmerised; it was some moments before she spoke.

'But I thought you said it was a man?'

'Yes I thought it was, Jono referred to her as Tony, so I assumed she was male. It turns out she was known as Toni.'

'So, what was she doing at Hell's Drop?' asked Lizzie evenly.

'Good question,' replied Jim.

'Did no one realise she hadn't returned home? I mean you might notice if I went off and didn't come back – well, eventually anyway,' said Lizzie trying to sound casual and inject a small amount of black humour into the exchange to lighten the atmosphere.

'It seems she was a bit of a free spirit. She had had a lot of jobs; the insurance selling was just one in a long line. She had told Jono the last time she saw him that she was planning to go to Greece or maybe it was Portugal, he couldn't quite remember which, to sell timeshare apartments, so he wasn't too surprised when he didn't hear from her; she had drifted in and out of his life for years. I think at one time he had hoped ... but then she made it clear she wasn't interested, so I think his enthusiasm for her waned a bit. Don't know if her parents reported her missing, or if they are still alive even. I don't know any more details yet.'

'My goodness, well that's awful; truly awful. I suppose she was staying in this area and walked out on her own and slipped. Easily done if you are not an experienced walker and haven't taken notice of the conditions,' said Lizzie, smoothing her hands down the front of her jeans as she got up and walked towards the door. 'Thank heavens she has been found, she can be laid to rest now I hope – poor girl.'

'That is just it,' said Jim flatly. 'Don't go back downstairs just yet Lizzie. I need to talk this through with you. She didn't appear to be staying in the area and she wasn't known for her enjoyment of outdoor pursuits, so why was she around here, if not to see me?'

'Jim that is a ridiculous assumption to make and has no foundation – the idea is ludicrous! Firstly, we don't know the time scale; it could have been months after she was supposed to make contact with you. She might have gone to Greece or wherever and come back. Secondly, there could be a hundred and one reasons why she was in the area, she wouldn't have come here just to see you would she, she probably had other clients hereabouts or maybe she was seeing a friend nearby. Thirdly ...'

'Yes, Lizzie I appreciate what you are saying,' interrupted Jim, 'but the fact is I have some information that I need to give the police. What they make of it is up to them. But I have seen too much death not to appreciate the value of life and I will do anything I can to help get some sort of closure for that poor girl's family. I am going to ring them now.'

Lizzie realised she really could not protest any further. She watched Jim walk over to the phone. She returned to the bar downstairs, her mind in turmoil.

When Jim came downstairs he told her he had made an appointment to see Gary Carmichael, who was now a detective constable in Keswick, the following day. Now that Antonia's identity had been confirmed a picture had been procured by the press and no doubt because she was quite attractive, it had made the daily newspapers and an item on the TV news.

A senior detective held a press conference, appealing for information however insignificant. A photo of her car or one like it was produced and her number plate displayed. A few reporters had started to drift around the village and apparently were also in Rowendale asking if anyone could give them any information. An inquest was opened and adjourned by the coroner after formal identification of the body to give the authorities time to establish a cause of death and a possible timeframe.

*

Naomi Watts, Jim's former landlady, came into the pub the following lunchtime and asked Lizzie if she could have a few words in private. She was a small roundish elderly lady who did not walk easily. Lizzie took her through to the office but did not offer her a seat; she wanted this to be brief as Naomi did rather get on her nerves.

'I hardly like to mention this really Lizzie, but then it is bothering me so I thought I should,' said Naomi, licking her lips.

'Yes of course Naomi, what is it?' asked Lizzie impatiently, noting the indeterminate stains on the front of her jersey and thinking that Naomi's personal hygiene was leaving a bit to be desired these days; it must be a week or more since she had washed her hair from the look of it.

'Well dear, do you remember I spoke to you the day that Seth died and I was off to call the vet again – oh my poor Seth – you were having a bonfire? I told you I was sure I had seen you driving a different car the day previous. But you said no, I was mistaken and I didn't think about it anymore. I was in a terrible state about Seth after all. But you see I remembered the number plate and when I saw the TV with a picture of that poor girl, well ...' she paused.

'I know I am not expressing this very well, but you see Lizzie it was the number plate that made me take notice. Part of it was CW, my dear brother's initials – Cyril Watts – I noticed it when the car drove past me at the time and then again yesterday evening on the news, there were those same letters in the number plate CW. I don't know what make of car it was but it was a sort of yellow colour I do remember that, similar to the one in the picture the policeman had. Then of course there's the question of what you were burning on your bonfire. You see it looked to me like clothes. Why would you do that rather than give them to charity? You can see my dilemma can't you Lizzie dear. You are so very precious to me and so kind, yet I feel it is my duty to report what I saw.'

'Naomi, the car in question was a hatchback I believe and I have never driven such a car, in fact I really cannot even recall the day you are thinking of. If I was having a bonfire then it was probably because a lot of rubbish had accumulated; there may have been some old rags as well but that's hardly noteworthy surely? You yourself have just said you were in a state about Seth, so you probably weren't thinking straight. The mind can play tricks when we are stressed. However, as you say, the police did suggest that anyone with any information, however time-consuming and irrelevant should come forward, so please do so. I'm sure they will be delighted to hear from you. In fact come on, let's do it now, no time like the present. I'll dial the number for you.'

Lizzie did not know what else to do, other than call Naomi's bluff. She marched purposefully to the phone and picked up the receiver.

'Oh, no, now I'm getting flustered Lizzie. I cannot be totally sure and of course – as you say it was a long time ago and I really don't want to get involved with the police. Your word is good enough for me; I just wanted some advice about the right thing to do. As I said, I do value your friendship so very dearly, I would hate to give you any unnecessary worry or get you mixed up with a police enquiry; that wouldn't be very good for business I am sure. No I'll leave it. Friends should stick together shouldn't they?'

'Yes my dear, I think they should and I too value your friendship,' said Lizzie with as much sincerity as she could muster as she put her arm around the rather malodorous form of Naomi Watts, trying not to inhale as she did so.

'We must make sure we see more of each other,' said Naomi hopefully, 'it gets quite lonely in my little cottage at times.'

'I am sure it does and I think we should do something about that. Come and have a drink in the bar this evening and we will arrange a girly day out to Carlisle, or Keswick if you would prefer.'

'Oh Lizzie, yes please! I would love that,' said Naomi as she clapped her hands together and smiled, revealing slightly rotten teeth; her stale breath wafting in Lizzie's face. Lizzie turned away almost imperceptibly as she tried not to breathe in.

And so it began. To the amazement of the outside world Lizzie Lockwood and Naomi Watts became best friends.

*

Jim duly attended the police station and he seemed to be gone for hours Lizzie thought. Surely they couldn't suspect he had anything to do with the death. He finally came home and seemed a bit shaken by the experience. He said they had questioned him closely about any connection he had to the deceased; he could only tell them the truth; that actually he had none other than that she may have come to the area to see him but if so, she hadn't made contact. Jim said that finally they seemed to believe him.

The next day Lizzie herself was asked to attend the police station to give a statement, confirming that she had not seen or spoken to the dead woman.

Detective Constable Gary Carmichael said he remembered her well. Lizzie thought about the day he had come to the Blenthorne Inn to tell her that Richard had been fatally injured in a road traffic accident; he had been a PC at the time. He had a kind face, she had decided a long time ago that he was a decent sort of chap.

'Thank you for coming in Lizzie. Please take a seat.'

'I would have said it's nice to see you under more pleasant circumstances Gary, however that doesn't really appear to be the case does it,' said Lizzie easily. 'Congratulations though on your transfer to CID.'

'Thank you, yes it pleased Cheryl. I was quite happy being a PC but she has ambition for me. She wants me to take my sergeant's exam now!'

'And so you should if you feel the time is right,' replied Lizzie giving him one of her nicest smiles.

He went through the motions of taking her statement, during which she confirmed that she had not seen Antonia Mason at any time or spoken to her on the phone; to her knowledge Antonia had never visited the Blenthorne Inn and she could shed no light on how she came to be found a few miles from their home.

The only vague connection was that prior to getting married, Jim had planned to consult a financial advisor regarding the possibility of taking out life insurance, on a recommendation from his old army mate and now business associate, George Johnson. Neither she nor Jim made any connection between that and the discovery of the remains found at Hell's Drop until Jono had rung them. Jim immediately contacted the police after taking the call.

As Gary saw Lizzie out she suggested he should come to Blenthorne for a drink or meal sometime with Cheryl.

She mentioned the restaurant was doing well and asked if the station had got its next Christmas party organised, she would make sure they got a very good rate if they wanted to come to Lockwood's. She promised to drop a leaflet in to the station next time she was in the area or alternatively he could visit the website. She said this with a flourish – she was still slightly in awe of the whole computer thing.

Lizzie hoped that she had satisfied the police and would not hear from them again. It was in fact a nice morning's work she thought as she drove home. She went in to make a statement and came out hoping she had secured the police station's Christmas party at least for this year.

As it turned out, she didn't need to drop a promotional leaflet at the police station, as Gary and two colleagues came to the pub a few days later. He told her that he had indeed visited the website and was going to bring Cheryl for a meal at the restaurant the following week. If that went well, as nominated social secretary for the station, he planned to make a booking for Christmas. She made a fuss of them and bought drinks all round. Maggie had told her afterwards that Gary had asked her about Antonia Mason but just in passing, nothing formal. She told him the truth; she had never to her knowledge seen the lady. Lizzie thanked her.

After investigating the matter thoroughly the forensic team could not say for certain what had happened to Antonia Mason. She has clearly been dead for some time when she was found; her head injuries were extensive and she had other injuries possibly consistent with a fall from Hell's Drop.

However evidence taken from those that knew her suggested it would have been out of character for her to go fell walking; particularly on her own to such an isolated spot.

The inquest was reconvened and in the absence of any clear evidence to the contrary, an open verdict was recorded. The case would remain on the police files and if new evidence should come to light at a future date, an active investigation would follow.

Lizzie hoped that would be the end of it. The only fly in the ointment was Naomi Watts, surely she could not live too much longer, she must be mid-eighties if she was a day and she had been in poor health for years. In fact it must be ten years since she had given up her farm. Soon Lizzie would be safe and this would all be behind her.

*

Lizzie was justified in her optimism regarding future patronage from the police. Gary's favourable report regarding the quality of the food after his meal with Cheryl had clearly had a positive influence. As time went by and word got round, Lockwood's became the place to celebrate any special occasion for officers and their families. The local constabulary's Christmas party venue was also sorted for the foreseeable future and Lizzie had been told that the assistant chief constable was to be seen now and again entertaining guests at Lockwood's.

All was looking right with the world once more, or so Lizzie thought, even if she did look over her shoulder from time to time.

It was a good thing that she could not see into the future.

Chapter 8

Naomi – 2003

Life had changed a little as Alex had nearly finished his catering college course and was spending more and more time with his girlfriend Faye. They were planning to move to a cottage owned by some friends of Faye's parents a couple of miles north of Blenthorne. So the dynamic had altered for Lizzie and Jim and they had to get used to Alex not being around so much.

Lizzie had been worried that Jim might miss Alex, that maybe he was the glue that held them together. However, after a bit of emotional readjustment on Lizzie's part, she realised that their relationship was as strong as ever. They were busy people but each evening they sat in companionable good humour as they discussed the events of the day and any plans for the future. It wasn't as if they didn't still see Alex regularly, he was working part time just across the drive after all. He and Jim remained as close as if they had a blood tie. Alex too planned to join the local volunteer fell rescue team and was doing his bit within the community with fundraising, which was extending to his old primary school in Rowendale where Faye was now a reception class teacher.

Finally Lizzie had got the bathroom fittings in their flat changed to a white suite with a separate shower cubicle. The avocado en suites in the guest rooms had also at last been consigned to history and not before time. However, guests came back time and time again in spite of the avocado and in fact one was heard to comment that he actually missed the ambience the ageing bathroom fittings gave the place. Lizzie told him that had she known that he was so attached to the sanitary ware, she would have saved it for him to take home!

They were just laughing about some guests who stayed with them year after year and sadly had divorced. Both parties still wanted to come for a holiday each year to the Blenny, so a compromise had been reached. Lizzie had conspired with them in the formulation of a code to ensure they were never in residence at the same time. So the room would be "in the process of redecoration" should one wish to book a room while the other was staying. This seemed to work well, but Jim did get rather mixed up and recently when he answered the phone he had told the ex-wife and her new partner that they would probably prefer not to stay the week they had chosen as they might not like the company! The poor lady had been terribly confused.

The phone rang and Jim got up to answer it.

'One guess as to who that is at this hour!' He listened for a short time. 'It's for you, Naomi again – what this time I wonder?' he said ironically with his hand over the receiver.

Naomi had tried knocking at the door but they had locked up for the night, so she had gone to the phone box over the road. Really this was getting too much thought Lizzie. This time she wanted Lizzie to pop round as she thought her fridge freezer was playing up.

'I am so sorry to be a nuisance Lizzie dear, but do you think you could collect my frozen bits and keep them for me, as I am afraid they will thaw out if I leave it till morning. Of course I will need someone to come out and have a look at the freezer, although it is very old, so maybe I should get a new one, the problem is they are rather expensive aren't they, particularly when one is living on a pension.'

Lizzie collected her vexatious friend from outside the phone box and duly drove the short distance to the cottage and collected Naomi's frozen food – which consisted of two pork chops, a tub of ice cream and half a packet of frozen peas – and promised to take her into Keswick the following day to pick out a new fridge freezer.

Four long years had passed since Lizzie and Naomi had become best friends – possibly the longest years of Lizzie's life.

Naomi was an elderly lady in frail health; however since her friendship with Lizzie, she seemed to have taken on a new lease of life. They had girls' days out, shopped together and had lunch every week, if it was particularly cold and Naomi did not feel like leaving the warmth of her cottage, Lizzie did her shopping and dropped it round.

Lizzie had taken to doing Naomi's washing and ironing – "at least that way we can ensure she stays clean" Lizzie had told Jim when he queried why she had taken on yet another chore. She also helped Naomi with her spring cleaning and paid Tim Bumstead, Bert's son to decorate her house from top to bottom.

'Oh Lizzie I could not accept such generosity,' declared Naomi.

'Nonsense we are busy ladies, we do not have time for decorating, so get a man in, that's what I say,' said Lizzie wistfully and Naomi clapped her hands together in glee.

In fact it seemed that Lizzie was now having to pop round to Naomi's house on an almost daily basis to help with one little job or another.

She could cope with the demands – just – however Lizzie was getting worried. Naomi was becoming a liability.

She had overheard her a while ago holding audience in the pub, which in itself was fine – having a few local characters gave the place a certain charm. The regulars all knew her and felt she was part of the fabric of the Blenthorne; there had been Watts farming in the area for over a hundred years and Naomi was the last in the line.

She knew Naomi's older brother Cyril had been killed during the war; Lizzie thought in Sicily. He would have been expected to take over the farm and after his death Naomi had stayed on to help her parents, who never really recovered from losing him. Lizzie felt sorry for Naomi. Any chance she had of leaving and making a life away from this small place had been denied her by her unswaying devotion to her parents. Her mother had lived to be nearly ninety and along with taking care of the farm, Naomi had looked after her. She reminded herself of this daily whenever Naomi needed "another little favour".

That really made what had to be done so much harder. The problem was Naomi had now brought up the "incident" several times.

On the first occasion she was sitting close to a walker with whom she had got into conversation. As Lizzie collected glasses from a nearby table she clearly heard Naomi say:

'... and the body was discovered a few miles from here. Obviously I'm a loyal friend, so I can say no more ...' Lizzie was then called back to the bar by a regular who asked if it was possible to get a drink before he died of thirst. A rather unfortunate turn of phrase in the circumstances but Lizzie composed herself sufficiently to pull his pint with a smile and a friendly aside, as was her wont.

'I was going to say keep your hair on, however,' she surveyed his bald pate, 'it's a bit late for that isn't it Jack!' They laughed together and Lizzie's gaze turned to the table where Naomi had been sitting with her new friend. Thankfully he was making his excuses as his companion had returned from the direction of the toilets and they were extricating themselves as tactfully as possible.

On another occasion a few of the regulars were still drinking but things were dying down and Lizzie suggested that Naomi might like to be getting home as it was late. Jim offered to walk her back to her cottage as Lizzie could manage the last few customers. He didn't like the thought of Naomi possibly stumbling in the dark in view of the alcohol she had consumed, but he was too polite obviously to mention that.

'Why Jim, you aren't worried I might get murdered are you?' slurred Naomi.

'Of course not – why on earth would anyone want to murder you Naomi?' asked Jim quizzically.

'Well you never know do you. I mean who would want to murder that poor girl whose body was found near here a few years ago. What do you think Lizzie, who would murder an innocent girl like that?' asked Naomi, through whisky breath and saliva. There was a pause before she continued, 'I love you Lizzie Lockwood and I would never, ever do anything to hurt you or yours.' She wiped her mouth with the back of her left hand to remove the excess spittle.

'And I love you too Naomi Watts, now away with you woman and find your bed,' Lizzie exhaled and forced a smile at the elderly lady before her.

Naomi's health had been deteriorating for years. She had insulin dependent type I diabetes as well as osteoarthritis. The latter was the main reason that she had to give up the farm, her mobility had been decreasing and she did not have the funds to employ someone to do the manual labour that running a farm entailed.

In addition she apparently had several other less severe co-morbidities and drank far too much. So how on earth did she manage to keep going? Lizzie had visited her as usual on Tuesday afternoon to have tea and see if she needed anything. As they drunk their tea Naomi had said how things were becoming increasingly difficult to manage at home.

Lizzie had replied that it would be a shame if Naomi was no longer able to stay at her cottage and suggested that she could arrange for a phone to be installed so that Naomi could ring if she needed anything urgently and if she wanted, carers might come in on a daily basis.

'Of course if you would prefer Naomi, you might like to think about going into residential care – maybe just for respite to start with, to see if you like it. I have heard that Triple Dale Residential Home in Rowendale has an excellent reputation.' Please say yes, thought Lizzie as she held her breath.

'Actually Lizzie dear, I wondered, as long as it wouldn't be too much trouble of course, if I could maybe stay with you and Jim, at least for a little while. I do so love your company. You always make me so welcome, I feel as if I am part of your family and I enjoy sitting in the bar of an evening. If I had a room at the pub, I would not have to bother poor Jim to take me home.

'Not a guest room obviously – I wouldn't want to stop you from letting it out,' said Naomi clearly noting the look of horror on Lizzie's face. 'Just the one at the back in your flat that Alex used to have, I mean he doesn't need it really does he, now that he has practically moved in with Faye. A lovely girl, I have always liked the family – did I tell you I was at school with her grandfather? He married Elsie from Yew Tree Farm you know. Anyway, what was I saying? Oh yes – Alex's room – there would be enough space for my TV and maybe a couple of bits of my furniture if you took out the chest of drawers and wardrobe that are there at the moment.'

Lizzie was silent for several seconds.

'I would need to discuss it with Jim but Naomi, have you really thought it through, I mean there would be the noise from the bar, customers leaving the restaurant at all hours, particularly the large parties now that we have an extended licence.'

'You have a whole cottage at the moment to call your own. Surely you don't want to swap that for one small room?' said Lizzie hopefully.

'Well I would have one small room if I went to live at Triple Dale wouldn't I? You seemed to think that would be acceptable a moment ago,' replied Naomi sharply, looking expectantly at Lizzie with a small innocent smile playing around her lips.

The silence that followed was heavy and oppressive as the unspoken consequences of non-compliance with Naomi's wishes became clear.

'Okay dear, well leave it with me for now. I will talk to Jim and see what he thinks,' sighed Lizzie in absolute dismay.

She thought afterwards that was probably the moment she realised she could wait no longer for nature to take its course. She would have to give nature a helping hand.

*

She pondered how best to tackle the problem over the next few weeks. Naomi was no longer able to walk far because of her osteoarthritis, so suggesting a hike and picnic to Blen Tarn during which a fatal fall might accidentally occur was not an option.

She also discounted a few rather far-fetched ideas such as trying to induce anaphylactic shock or maybe some form of sepsis through a dirty needle or possibly toxic mushrooms – well toadstools but then Naomi was a country girl, she would know the difference between a harmless mushroom and a poisonous toadstool.

However, time was short as Naomi was again pestering her for a decision on moving in. She had started a conversation about small cars in the bar the previous evening.

'Have you ever driven a little hatchback Lizzie ... No? Oh, my mistake, I thought you had.'

Really something had to be done and done quickly.

She had been laying down the preparatory work for a while, even before she had decided how to proceed. She had started spreading rumours in the bar – how easy it was. She just mentioned in passing that someone had told her Naomi Watts was becoming increasing forgetful. However, she really should not have said anything and please not to pass it on.

A few days later, Tom from the newsagents had told her in the strictest confidence that he had heard that Naomi Watts was going a bit funny in the head and getting confused.

The idea of the needle had led her to thinking about Naomi's insulin regime. She knew Naomi injected herself with a pen device to keep her levels stable. This could be her answer. She could maybe induce a state of diabetic ketoacidosis, a condition which can occur in patients whose management is suboptimal and their control poor. She was dredging her memory for the exact process from her nursing days and she would need to read up on it as she had to get it right first time.

When Tom next came in, she managed to bring Naomi into the conversation and said she was worried by what he had told her the other day and confided in him that Naomi had got muddled with her blood sugar readings when she was visiting her. However, that was told in the strictest confidence.

A few days later she had seen Sally Barton a local farmer when she stopped off to buy some stamps at the post office. Sally told her that apparently Naomi was getting forgetful and possibly in the early stages of dementia, she had heard that sometimes she was not taking her medication properly. However, that was told in the strictest confidence.

Lizzie decided she had sufficiently paved the way and it was now time to put the end game in motion.

She visited Naomi and said that after a long discussion with Jim they would be delighted for her to move in with them. In fact they were going to get Alex's old bedroom sorted and when it was all finished she could move her bits and pieces in and they would live together, just as a proper family should. Naomi was thrilled.

'Oh Lizzie I can't thank you enough,' she gushed. 'I won't be any trouble.'

No, you won't, thought Lizzie grimly.

Lizzie told Jim that night that she had sort of promised that Naomi could move in with them. She said that she was frankly beside herself with worry about Naomi who really could not be trusted to take care of herself. She feared what would happen if they did not take her in.

'Yes I know Lizzie, and I do like her – well "like" is a bit strong; I don't dislike her but at the end of the day she really is not our responsibility. I mean, you would not have your mother living with us would you – yet you are prepared to take in someone whom I am not really convinced that you particularly like.'

'That's totally different, my mother has my father,' said Lizzie, her voice unusually high in tone. 'Call me gullible if you like. Maybe I am a pushover and let people take advantage of me. The problem is, if I see someone in trouble, I can't just cross over and walk on the other side; maybe I should Jim, maybe I'm stupid to want to help those less fortunate than myself.'

Lizzie was sure Jim knew exactly to what she was alluding. He had been in a bad way when she had benevolently given him a job.

'I'm sorry. You must do as you think best. Your kindness does you credit,' said Jim quietly as he hugged her briefly and left the room. Lizzie did have the good grace to blush.

*

The next day Lizzie went to see Naomi with a bottle of whisky tucked in her bag.

'It's a bit early even for me!' said Naomi as she struggled from her chair and got two glasses out of the sideboard.

'We deserve a little treat I think,' said Lizzie. They sat together in the cottage for a couple of hours as Naomi talked of the old days, her friends, most of whom were now dead, her family and the farm as she steadily had her glass refilled by Lizzie who remained completely sober.

She chatted about the changes to the community and the incomers who had sold up and moved from their city homes to take up residence in Lakeland for an idyllic lifestyle.

'Not quite so idyllic in the winter when the rain doesn't stop for days on end and a heavy veil of mist shrouds the hills or we get snowed in for weeks,' chuckled Naomi.

'Well I am sure they all have central heating and large freezers, so they can prepare for siege conditions and remain indoors until the worst is over,' laughed Lizzie. 'As long as they stagger along to the pub and buy a drink or two, I am not complaining.'

Naomi was settled happily into her chair and dropping off to sleep. Lizzie moved as silently as possible to the kitchen. She opened the fridge and took out one box of Naomi's spare insulin cartridges. In the kitchen drawer she located one of the small orange needles used for subcutaneous injections. After years of helping Naomi with "little jobs" she knew exactly where everything was kept.

She worked quickly and efficiently, her purpose clear. She decided to alter several insulin cartridges in case Naomi chose to change the one Lizzie planned to give her. She took out the cartridges and used the fine needle to draw off the insulin from each and tipped it down the sink, washing it away as she went. Every now and then she glanced up out of the window to make sure no one was on the pathway delivering anything to the cottage – she would have a hard time explaining what she was doing if she was spotted.

She then filled the needle with water which she injected through the tight mesh wire covering each cartridge. This was a painstaking process and several times Lizzie went to check that Naomi was still asleep. However, she was well away and Lizzie went up to the bedroom and got a blanket to cover her with so that she did not wake because she was cold.

When she had finished her laborious task she returned the box of cartridges to the fridge. She then went back to the living room and removed Naomi's current insulin pen which was lying on the small table near to her, next to her library book, blood glucose meter, glasses and the lamp.

She went into the kitchen and made Naomi an omelette before waking her. She returned to the living room with a tray containing the omelette and a mug of tea.

'Naomi dear, my goodness, we both dropped off, that will teach us – boozing in the afternoon!' Lizzie set the tray down on the nearby dining table.

'Oh Lizzie how kind and thoughtful you are. I just need to check my sugar levels.'

'Let me help you dear. Where is your insulin pen?'

'Oh I am not sure, isn't it there?'

'No dear, I think you said you needed to start a new cartridge anyway. I will get one of your spares out and pop a new cartridge in for you.' She left the room and got one of the sabotaged cartridges from the fridge. She took this and a new pen into the living room where Naomi was out of her chair and struggling to bend down to look under it for her existing pen.

'Not to worry Naomi, you have several spares,' said Lizzie as she helped Naomi to her feet.

'But I just can't think what I have done with it,' said Naomi.

'We all lose things; I lost my car keys the other day. Still haven't found them. I'm using the spare set at the moment. I will pop back and see you in the morning, as I think you are looking a little peaky,' said Lizzie briskly.

'You are so good to me Lizzie; I don't know what I would do without you.'

Lizzie left quickly and returned to the pub.

'Sorry,' she said to Jim as she walked through the door 'Naomi seemed a bit down, so I stayed with her and will pop back tomorrow.'

'You are an amazing woman Lizzie,' said Jim sincerely. Lizzie spent the evening in the kitchen preparing and cooking meals as the orders came through. She slept fitfully, it wasn't that she didn't have a conscience but she repeatedly told herself that what she was doing was necessary to stop Naomi from giving her away.

The next morning was bright and a little breezy; the village looked a tranquil and gentle place with the inhabitants completely unaware of the drama unfolding inside Naomi's cottage. Lizzie went to the door of the cottage and let herself in with the key Naomi had given her several years ago. Naomi was still in her chair with the half eaten omelette and an empty mug beside her.

'Naomi, what's wrong?' asked Lizzie.

'I don't know, I think my sugar levels must be playing up, I feel sick and I am awfully thirsty.'

'Let's get you to bed and I will check your levels and give you your insulin.' Lizzie assisted Naomi up to her bedroom and helped her undress. After this she checked her blood sugar levels and helped her with her insulin pen. She left this by the bed. She also gave her a few sips of water.

'Not too much, if you are nauseous you will not keep it down. I will pop back later Naomi, now you stay in bed until you feel better. Such a shame you don't have a phone, otherwise you could ring me if you feel any worse.'

Lizzie left after collecting the crockery and tray from the living room and washing up. On returning to the pub she told Jim that Naomi was much better and talking about having a sort through her things before her move. The morning passed smoothly and she returned to the cottage after the lunchtime rush.

Naomi was breathing heavily and as Lizzie approached the bed she could smell pear drops on her breath, the tell-tale sign that ketones were rising in Naomi's blood. Lizzie knew that the body starts to burn fatty acids if it has no insulin and this produces acid ketone bodies. She noted that the process was taking hold, just as it should. Lizzie used the glucose testing meter to establish that Naomi was hyperglycaemic. She did not have a sphygmometer but was hopeful that Naomi's blood pressure was dropping, in accordance with the other symptoms of the condition she was trying to induce.

'Naomi dear; can you hear me?'

'Oh Mummy, where have you been? I have been calling you.'

Lizzie felt tears pricking her eyes. No going back now. She must not lose her nerve. Naomi was clearly confused.

'I have such a pain in my tummy, can I have the pink medicine please. What time will Daddy be home today? Where is Cyril?'

'You will see them both soon dear, very soon – sleep now,' Lizzie whispered. She felt sick at what she was allowing to happen but told herself she had no choice.

Again upon her return she told Jim that Naomi was fine and she need not visit until the day after tomorrow.

Lizzie suggested to Jim that they treat themselves to an outing the next day. They rose early and followed their normal morning routine, leaving just after Maggie arrived. She assured them she would be fine until Bert got there and Carl was also around. She told them to enjoy themselves, if anyone deserved a break it was Lizzie.

They made for Helm Crag, a fell to the north of Grasmere. The walk would only take a couple of hours but they could have a leisurely lunch in the town before returning to Blenthorne to set up for the evening. Lizzie tried to put all thoughts of Naomi as far from her mind as possible.

The following day she let herself into the cottage and crept quietly upstairs into Naomi's bedroom.

'Naomi, how are you feeling?'

Naomi moaned slightly. Her breathing was coming in harsh painful gasps. Lizzie left the room and went down to the kitchen and removed the insulin cartridges she had tampered with, leaving the remainder in place. She then went back to the bedroom and substituted the original insulin pen she had taken from Naomi's small fireside table for the one she had given her as a replacement. She would dispose of the contaminated cartridges by shoving them in with the glass breakages from the pub.

She left the cottage as quietly as she could. On returning to the pub she told Jim she would look in tomorrow, as she was not convinced that Naomi was complying with her insulin regime properly, let alone taking her other medication.

'Well she will be living with us soon, so you will be able to supervise her. She is a lucky lady!' said Jim ironically.

Not so very lucky thought Lizzie.

She went back to the cottage in the morning. Having checked that all was as she wished it, she left and slowly walked back to the pub where she rang the local GP surgery to advise that sadly Naomi Watts had died in her sleep.

*

Dr Ruth Baker called at the cottage after morning surgery. She was a large outdoorsy type person in her early fifties with dark hair streaked with grey escaping from the bun she habitually wore. Lizzie met her at the door.

'Can you tell me how Miss Watts has been recently, health-wise?' asked the doctor when she came back down the stairs from examining the body.

'She has been slowing up in recent years and I understand from the gossip in the village she was getting a bit muddled. She had certainly become rather forgetful recently and didn't always take her medication when she should,' said Lizzie shaking her head sadly.

'Yes, I see. There will have to be a post mortem of course,' said the doctor, 'but I suspect that we are looking at poor compliance. 'We regularly invited her for health checks at the surgery to monitor her but to little avail I'm afraid. It's all free and still people won't attend!'

'Naomi was old-school, Ruth,' said Lizzie. 'Her mother apparently hardly ever went near a doctor in her life and she lived to be nearly ninety, so Naomi followed her example.'

'I know I am not family but is there any chance you will be able to tell me the outcome of the post mortem?' asked Lizzie.

'Well of course there isn't any family is there, so certainly unofficially you can probably guess as well as I can as to the cause of her death. I think we are looking at a case of DKA. Toxicology will confirm if she was compliant with her insulin regime.'

'I blame myself,' said Lizzie, quite truthfully but then qualified the statement. 'If I had only acted sooner – I was becoming increasingly worried about Naomi and her ability to take care of herself; I had recently persuaded her to come to live with me and Jim so that I could make sure she was properly looked after. I was very fond of her,' said Lizzie simply with a quiver in her voice.

'Most people I know don't even want to look after their own relatives, let alone a neighbour,' said the doctor. 'That was so very kind of you Lizzie. This world would be a better place if there were more people like you in it,' she added as she squeezed Lizzie's arm. 'Try not to upset yourself; you did all you could for her.'

Lizzie had the good grace to feel rather embarrassed as she shook the doctor's hand and fought back her tears. She was actually going to miss the elderly lady in a strange sort of way.

As she left the cottage a dark cloud passed overhead obscuring the sun and Lizzie shivered involuntarily.

*

Over the next few weeks Lizzie felt that she should be able to relax again and wondered why she felt no sense of relief or elation.

The post mortem had passed off smoothly with the cause of death given by the pathologist as natural causes, just as the

GP predicted and there had been no need for an inquest. Naomi was cremated, with her ashes scattered near to her family in the local cemetery.

The whole village turned out to say goodbye. Naomi would have liked that. Lizzie and Jim hosted the wake at the pub and they all toasted a good long life and the person that had been Naomi Watts. Everyone said that Lizzie had looked after Naomi like a daughter. No one could have been kinder or more altruistic towards an elderly neighbour.

The will was read and it transpired that, having no family, Naomi Watts had left a few bequests to various charities and then everything she had in the world to Lizzie Lockwood in recognition of Lizzie's kindness and care towards her in the latter stages of her life.

Lizzie cried uncontrollably. What had she done?

If only Naomi had not seen her driving the car away from the pub on that fateful day. If only Naomi had not seen her stoking the bonfire the following morning. It was anchored in her mind because it was the day Seth died. Of course these events meant nothing to her at the time, but later when the remains were found and publicity revealed that Antonia had a gold hatchback registered to her, or yellow as Naomi had thought, Naomi had put two and two together. Even then, if Naomi had been reasonable things need not have come to a head.

Lizzie didn't mind the little favours Naomi asked of her, she was just lonely. It was only her time that Naomi wanted; there was never any suggestion of money, well not cash anyway. Hardly blackmail was it, not in the proper sense – she could have dealt with that. It was when Naomi had started blurting out inappropriate things that the problems started. Sooner or later someone would listen and when they did ...

There was surely no evidence after all this time, but what if Maggie suddenly remembered the paperweight covered in bits of brains that Lizzie had so foolishly missed when she was disposing of the body?

Thankfully the hatchback had never been found so she had not needed her Carlisle alibi after all. Lizzie had hoped by leaving the keys in the ignition an opportunistic thief would steal the car and presumably this is what had happened. They would hardly be likely to come forward would they? She had also left the shoes in the boot, but there was nothing to connect them with her even if someone had found them.

On the surface all seemed to be going well; their businesses were running smoothly with a steady increase in the profits. Carl was making a huge success of the restaurant with new ideas and promotions attracting trade from far and wide. She could leave that side of the business to him and Jim. The hotel was full most of the time with walkers or clients attending Windy and Jono's adventure holidays. And dear Jim had had no flashbacks for ages, bless him. They ran the pub together and seemed to be happier as time went by. He was not a tactile man, just there – kind and caring and everything she could ever want.

She had developed a skilful knack of swamping shadows from the past with positive thoughts of the good things in her life. No, there was nothing else that could go wrong, not after all this time. Naomi was the only loose end and she had gone now.

Alex and Faye were planning an engagement party soon and after that, in the fullness of time, would come a wedding and then maybe even grandchildren! Alex had just gained his catering qualification and was happily ensconced under Carl's tutelage at Lockwood's. Things could not be better thought Lizzie happily.

Yes she was a lucky woman with her loving extended family around her – and then one day a chance encounter changed everything. Just when she thought her problems were behind her, she visited the Fell View Hotel and Luke Farmer came into her life.

Little did Lizzie know it at the time, but that was where it all started to fall apart.

Chapter 9

Luke – 2004

Robin Corey who co-owned the Fell View Hotel was looking forward to his meeting with Lizzie arranged for later that morning, he was always excited by her business ideas. He and Mark Stevens had long wanted to give up their everyday jobs and run a hotel; they talked about it at length. He had been a manager for a fast food chain and Mark was a hairdresser. It was only when he had received a small inheritance from his grandmother that they had enough for a deposit; this made their dream possible but they did need additional capital and had to take out a substantial mortgage; at the time it seemed lenders were falling over themselves to offer money.

The repayments meant it was difficult for them to afford to employ sufficient staff but without extra help they could not give a good enough service. Also, although the structure of the building was sound, the fabric was in need of updating. Their running costs meant that they had inadequate funds to address this. They had almost resigned themselves to failure anyway and then a national hotel chain purchased a similar establishment in nearby Rowendale. They had thought that was the final straw. Given the choice, who would stay with them when they could get a far better deal just down the road? They saw their clientele dwindle, putting even more pressure on them to meet their mortgage commitments.

So his rather tongue in cheek approach to Lizzie that day a few years ago when he had asked her if she wanted to buy a hotel had been the saving of them. The partnership between the Lockwoods and himself and Mark worked well. The cash injection had been sufficient to get through their financial difficulties and with the trade generated by the adventure holidays, they were well in profit. They had not looked back since Lizzie and Jim had become partners. Robin tended to take care of the business side of things and Mark was more hands on with day-to-day running of the hotel.

They had redecorated; a good deal organised through Lizzie. Tim Bumstead was an excellent painter and decorator and he could also turn his hand to a bit of carpentry. The old 80s décor with its dado rails and two toned wallpaper was replaced with cool pastel shades with cream drapes and the large brass chandeliers gave way to gentle discrete lighting. In addition they changed the sagging slightly threadbare settees and armchairs, which had been accumulated over time and consequently did not match, with sleek smooth lined fabric sofas and armchairs in the lounge, all in complimentary shades to match the walls – again some influence from Lizzie. They had taken a leaf out of her book and gone for rugs and flagstone floors downstairs. So much cheaper to replace a rug than a carpet she had said, it only takes one accident and how right she was. With a revamping of the reception area and decorating the guest rooms bit by bit, they were well on the way to realising their dream.

Inevitably as business picked up, they needed to take on more bar staff; the first thing most clients from the adventure holiday scheme wanted after an action packed day, was a long cold drink. If they couldn't provide it, the customers would go elsewhere and who knows, even dine out – horror of horrors! This ate into their profits but they had to accept they could not run the bar by themselves. Norman their regular barman for the last year had decided to retire as his wife was poorly and they had just taken on a new chap, Luke Farmer.

Robin was looking out for Lizzie and planned to be on the doorstep to greet her as usual. Then the phone rang – he had better get that, it could be a booking and Karen, their usual receptionist, was having a day off. Her assistant Misty – what sort of a name was that? – was worse than useless, he would have to do something about her; all smiles and nails but nothing behind the eyes or it seemed between the ears.

They were usually good judges of character he thought, however both he and Mark had got it wrong in her case. On that tack, he really must speak to Luke again about his references. He had been with them for over three weeks and Robin had had to ask him twice to provide any at all and now he had taken them up, neither had replied – well he supposed he should give it a bit longer. It was not that Luke wasn't a good worker and of course very polite, but there was something about him that Robin could not quite put his finger on.

Lizzie arrived that sunny June morning to see Robin about the possibility of the hotel applying for a wedding licence. Legislation had come into force some time ago and Lizzie felt it was quite a lucrative idea, particularly if they could incorporate some outdoor pursuits, courtesy of Jono and Windy, to make each wedding package a blend of dynamic entertainment and calm relaxation prior to the main event. On the big day itself, every detail from the pre-ceremony drinks to cutting the cake would be taken care of.

The venue was superb with fantastic views, as the name suggested, across the nearby fells. There was a large reception room which could be used for ceremonies and twenty five en suite rooms for wedding guests. For larger parties, Lizzie had said she was sure a few of the local B&B owners would be interested in coming on board – she could organise that if the boys wanted her to, as she knew everyone in the village. It could be a real money spinner. Yes, Robin really was looking forward to seeing Lizzie and now he was stuck on the blasted phone!

*

As she arrived at the hotel Lizzie saw a youngish chap, roughly late twenties or early thirties behind the bar. He was quite tall with a slim build and neatly cropped dark hair. No tattoos or piercings, Lizzie was pleased to see.

'Hello, I'm here to see Robin – I'm Lizzie Lockwood, are you new?' She extended her hand and smiled. He took it and looked at her quizzically.

'Good to meet you. Yes – Luke Farmer – I started three weeks ago. I was working in Carlisle before but decided I needed a change of scene and ended up here. I will get Robin for you, please excuse me.'

He left and returned a minute later to suggest that Lizzie could go to the office as Robin was currently on the phone. He walked with her, which although polite, Lizzie thought was rather unnecessary as she knew the way but it seemed that he wanted to talk to her.

'Have we met before Lizzie; it's just that you seem familiar somehow?' said Luke.

'Possibly,' said Lizzie which was her usual stock answer designed not to offend but also to convey that she did not recognise the person questioning her. 'I do meet a lot of people in my line of work – I run the Blenthorne Inn just up the road.'

'Oh, yes, maybe that's it,' said Luke, clearly not convinced.

Robin rushed out of the office to meet Lizzie.

'Darling, I am so sorry,' he said in his usual gushing manner as he kissed her on both cheeks. 'I was caught up on the phone when Luke said you were here. Come through – coffee – yes of course you will – Luke could you organise that for us please, coffee for two in the office and maybe a few biscuits – thanks.' Luke retraced his steps back to the bar still clearly trying to remember where he had seen Lizzie Lockwood before.

Lizzie and Robin had a very profitable meeting as usual and it was agreed that Robin would look into the possibility of a wedding licence and Lizzie would speak to Jim regarding organising a recreational package to be run by Jono and Windy and the necessary marketing. They always seemed to be on the same wavelength which made their business working relationship very easy and their friendship a natural result of that. Robin saw Lizzie to the door.

'Oh Robin, I know how busy he is but do you think Mark would have time to do my roots later this week?' asked Lizzie.

'For you, anything – I will get him to give you a ring. I'm sure that can be arranged – heaven forfend, we can't have you on display with your roots showing, what would your public think!' joked Robin as he waved her off.

*

'Nice lady,' said Luke as Robin came back through the bar area.

'Yes, she is lovely; wonderfully public spirited. Would do anything for anyone; too kind for her own good really. Goodness knows what this village would do without her,' said Robin.

'That's nice to know,' said Luke thoughtfully as he slowly polished a glass. He had just remembered where he had seen her before. It was some time ago, years in fact, but he was sure it was her. If that were true then he was sitting on dynamite! The question was, what was he going to do about it?

He smiled to himself. Maybe he would not have to stay here that much longer, short changing customers in the bar when he got the chance and checking if any of the guests had left their bedroom doors unlocked so that he could see if they had anything worth pinching.

Mark seemed okay but that damned Robin was on his case constantly about his references. He thought he had done a pretty good job on them, but unfortunately Robin had insisted on taking them up. Well he would be waiting a long time for replies. So all in all, this had come at just the right time.

Just maybe all his Christmases and birthdays had come at once. He could conduct a bit of business with the saintly Mrs Lizzie Lockwood and be on his way – well at least until he needed a bit more money, then he would contact her again.

She had said she was pleased to meet him; he doubted she would feel that way for long.

*

'Lizzie there is a chap in the bar asking after you,' called Bert from the public bar.

'Okay I'll be there in a minute,' answered Lizzie from the kitchen. They had taken on someone to do the evening catering now as Jim said really she should not need to be cooking all the time; however she enjoyed it and found it difficult not to help – or interfere as Jim put it. It was rather painful for her as this part of the enterprise was very much her baby and she just needed to keep an eye on it.

She walked into the public bar and saw a young man sitting just to the right of the beer pumps.

'Hello Lizzie,' he said in what Lizzie felt was a rather overfamiliar tone. 'Good to see you again.'

'Sorry, have we met – oh yes of course, you work for Robin and Mark don't you. Luke isn't it. I remember now, you were behind the bar when I came over the other day. Nice to see you here; having a night off?'

'Yes I have had the whole day off actually; been over the Carlisle. Nice place. Have you ever been there?'

'Well yes of course I have, it's the largest shopping centre in the area. I don't suppose anyone that has lived here for more than a few months has not been to Carlisle! Why do you ask?' asked Lizzie her head slightly on one side thinking what a strange question it was.

'Well I have just remembered where I saw you before. It was several years ago, in a car park. Do you remember?' asked Luke sipping his pint and placing the glass on the beer mat very carefully.

He folded his arms and leant forward on the bar, a small rather unpleasant smile playing around the corners of his mouth, he started to sway gently backwards and forwards. Bert was hovering close by in a protective sort of way.

Lizzie exhaled a little

'Um, well, no sorry I don't. I usually leave my car in one of the central car parks depending on available spaces and I probably see quite a few people when I am doing so. On that basis I don't think it is too surprising that I can't remember you. Why on earth would you remember me?' asked Lizzie puzzled.

'I will let you think about it for a few days,' said Luke. He then drained his pint in one go and placed the glass back on the mat. 'I'll be in touch – so long.' With that he left.

'What was that all about?' asked Bert as he walked closely behind her on his way to serve a customer at the far end of the bar.

'I wish I knew,' said Lizzie with a vague sense of unease.

Lizzie did wonder about contacting Robin and Mark about their choice of barman, but she didn't want to make a fuss. It was probably just some sort of attempt to feign a connection where there wasn't one, although why he should want to, Lizzie could not imagine. Unless of course ... but no, that was years ago. Leaving the hatchback in Carlisle – could he have seen her and remembered – she doubted it. Well even if he did, she had an alibi – she had kept her return bus tickets until Naomi had passed away and it was possible they were still in a drawer somewhere. She would just stick to her story that he was mistaken.

She wondered why she did not feel as confident as she would like.

*

Two days later, true to his word, Luke made contact. He must have been hanging around outside, as when she went to her car he seemed to appear from nowhere and approached her from behind. She jumped involuntarily as he spoke to her. He was far too close for comfort.

'Hi Lizzie. Sorry if I made you jump – have you had a chance to remember our meeting yet? Well to be honest it wasn't really a meeting because we didn't actually speak. I was a couple of metres from you when you left your car – at least when I took it I thought it was your car – however it turns out it belonged to that woman who was found dead. Do you remember? Her body was discovered a few years back quite near here – now isn't that a coincidence? You dump her car and she turns up dead. I did think it strange behaviour to not lock the car – second nature really isn't it, like flushing the bog. But never look a gift horse in the mouth, so I didn't hang around to wonder why you hadn't locked it. Mind you, even if you had I could have still taken it. I'm good at that you see.'

'How very nice for you Luke; your mother must be so proud. I have absolutely no idea what you are talking about or who you are mistaking me for but I can assure you that it was not me you saw leaving a car in Carlisle with the keys in the ignition.'

'Oh dear, oh dear Lizzie – I never mentioned leaving the keys in the ignition did I? Of course that would be why you could not lock the door wouldn't it, because they were on the same fob.' Luke said sarcastically.

Shit! thought Lizzie.

'Semantics,' she said quickly.

'You what?' said Luke clearly puzzled by the word.

'You are playing with words,' she said hoping she sounded convincing. 'If you think you have some information regarding me, I suggest you take it to the police; I understand the investigation into the death to which you're referring is still open. Goodbye Luke. Hopefully we won't meet again so have a nice life as they say.'

Lizzie got into her car and drove away, resisting the temptation to put her foot down. She looked in the mirror and saw him looking after her with his hands tucked firmly in his jeans pockets.

The next day he rang her mobile. For a long time she had resisted the temptation to have one but had given in finally. She was still not sure how to answer it, as she had only had it for a week and both Alex and Jim had shown her several times but it was all still a bit of a mystery. Anyway, this time she managed it.

'Hello again Lizzie, how are you today? It's Luke, in case you were wondering.'

'How did you get this number?' asked Lizzie sharply, her mind suddenly alert to danger.

'Robin had it – hope you don't mind me ringing you. I thought we could come to some arrangement. I don't want anything much from you, just a reference and a bit to tide me over until I find a job or another source of income.'

'I tell you what Luke, I'll meet you and we can discuss it. The centre of Keswick by the clock tower tomorrow at noon,' said Lizzie.

'Now that is a very sensible attitude and I knew you were a lady who would know what's best for her,' said Luke smugly as he rang off.

*

Lizzie had a plan of her own. She had thought half-heartedly about the possibility of somehow arranging an accident for Luke but it was not always that simple. He was not an unsuspecting woman with her back towards her or a frail elderly lady. She just didn't have the time to think of any other solution than the one she decided on. No, this was a dangerous ploy but it might work, if not, she was done for anyway, she could never explain away why she was driving Antonia's car.

She was getting tired of always looking over her shoulder; it was like trying to plug a hole in a boat, only for another to spring open. Just as she thought she had dealt with one problem another reared its ugly head; she had to end this once and for all – whatever the outcome.

*

The next day Lizzie was waiting by the clock tower as planned. Luke arrived a couple of minutes after noon with the collar of his denim jacket turned up; very theatrical thought Lizzie ironically.

'Hello Lizzie, it's really nice to see you again; so what have you got for me?' asked Luke.

'Well Luke I am sure it's something you'll be pleased about. I suggested you contact the police if you thought you had some information they would be interested in. It seemed to me that you were rather reluctant to do that, so I have done it for you. Let me introduce you to Detective Sergeant Gary

Carmichael. He will take you to the police station and you can tell him exactly what you have told me.'

Gary had been standing around the other side of the building and stepped forward with a pseudo-pleasant smile on his face. He somehow managed to give the appearance of looming over Luke though actually he was probably only a little taller.

'Hello Luke, would you like to come along with me and we can have a chat? I have been making a few enquiries about you; it seems you have got a bit of a penchant for other people's possessions – how many stretches have you done for breaking and entering to date? Turning your hand to a bit of blackmail now are you? I think you've picked the wrong victim this time mate, but I am very interested in what you have got to say for yourself.'

Before he could say any more Luke had turned and sprinted off along Market Place in the direction of Station Street. Gary turned and started to follow but Lizzie called him back. He returned to where she was standing.

'Let him go Gary, he's not worth the effort,' said Lizzie, very pleased with this outcome.

'I will put out an alert, hopefully we may well get him before he leaves the town,' said Gary.

'No honestly Gary, he is just a nasty opportunist little lowlife who thought he could tap me for some money – he's gone now so please let it go,' pleaded Lizzie as she placed her hand on Gary's arm.

'Up to you, I would be happy to see if we can apprehend him?'

Lizzie shook her head.

'Well at the very least I will have a chat with the owners of Fell View Hotel to see if they have had any reported thefts, Lizzie. But we can certainly get him on attempted blackmail if nothing else. We will catch up with him soon, don't worry. He won't stop you know, crime is a way of life for him, so even if we don't make an arrest today, it won't be long before he slips up and when he does we will have him.'

'Really, there has been no harm done, I just wanted him to tell you if he thought he had some information about a stolen car I think it was – I'm not really sure – he was a very strange young man. I would prefer just to forget the whole thing if you don't mind. How's Cheryl?'

'Wouldn't know; she has traded me in for a new model. Daft thing is she wanted me to go for my sergeant's exam and when I passed it and got a promotion to Carlisle, she left anyway! Living with a DCI she met at a dinner at your place actually. Poor chap – she probably has him in line for chief constable.'

Lizzie smiled at Gary's ironic joke.

'Oh Gary, I'm sorry, life can be tough sometimes, I do hope you see the boys regularly?'

'Oh yes, she is very good about that. Thank you for calling me Lizzie; I'm glad you felt you could come to me with this. Tell you what, I'll come over soon and have a drink if you and Jim would join me?'

'Oh yes we'd love to – in fact I will give you a ring next week and we will arrange dinner, take care Gary. Oh and Gary, please could you not mention this to anyone you don't have to, only I don't want everyone to know I was targeted by a petty criminal,' said Lizzie as she fished her car keys out of her bag and turned towards the direction of the car park.

'Of course, I will have to file a report, but that is all if you're sure you don't want to take it any further – at least unless I get any information from his employers. If that's the case, we will need to actively pursue him. Not that he will be too bothered I'm sure, occupational hazard for someone of his ilk. Take care Lizzie and don't forget anything I can do for you, anything at all, any time,' said Gary as he looked after Lizzie.

She left him with a smile and a wave and as she turned the corner towards the car park.

*

As she returned home she wondered if this audacious plan had actually worked. Too many times before she thought she was safe only to find she was not. Thank heavens for Gary Carmichael. She knew he had a soft spot for her and hopefully her double bluff had been sufficient to see Luke Farmer off – but was it enough to be rid of him for good?

She stopped off at Fell View to see Robin and Mark and catch up on how things were with them. Robin had already made the enquiries necessary to set in motion the wedding licence application, so there was much to do and much to plan for. As usual they made a huge fuss of her, insisting on tea and cake.

She flicked through a newspaper lying on the coffee table in front of where they were sitting in the corner of the lounge and something caught her eye. She saw a picture of a couple she recognised, the woman in particular, smiling up at her from the page. They were wearing evening clothes and looking very refined and dignified. The caption underneath told her that the newly knighted Sir Ashley Duncan and his wife Sarah were attending a dinner for business leaders given by the Prime Minister and that Sir Ashley was to become a government adviser shortly. She wondered if Jim had seen it – even if he had, she doubted he would mention it. His ex-wife was a closed subject between them.

Sarah's words from the party at Sheila's house echoed in her mind: "Look after Jim. He means the world to me". She remembered that Sarah had used the present tense rather than the past. Push the thought away. At the end of their meeting she got up to leave.

Just as she got to the door she turned and asked after Luke. 'I didn't seen him in the bar, is he having a day off?'

'Is he heck!' said Mark. 'Little toe rag had been short changing customers and I found him in the office the day before yesterday, rummaging through one of the drawers! Well we didn't want the publicity, so we let it go and didn't involve the police but we have got rid of him obviously.'

'Oh I see, well that's good, no real harm done then,' said Lizzie with a sigh. Sarah and Luke in the same day! She waved goodbye and drove home wearily.

She had an uneasy feeling that she had not heard the last of either Luke Farmer or Sarah Duncan.

Chapter 10

Gary – 2005

Gary Carmichael sat at his desk in the open plan office at the central police station in Carlisle. The time was approaching 8:30 p.m. Cheryl would have been hopping mad if he had still been at work at this hour when they were married. He hoped her new man managed to get home on time or he would be feeling the force of her wrath instead. At least now he didn't have that pressure but in a strange way he missed the nagging and he hated going home to an empty lifeless flat.

It had all started so well for them – he and Cheryl had so many plans for the future, then she discovered ambition, not for herself but for him. She was never happy with the house, the car, the holidays – even the children had turned out to be boys and she had wanted girls, so really he couldn't win. Finally he gave up trying and they had divorced after ten years of marriage. She had kept the house and they shared custody of the boys. He really looked forward to the time he spent with them every other weekend and alternate Wednesdays – apart from that he just worked. He ate at the station whenever possible and really only went to his flat to sleep and change his clothes.

His mind turned back to work. He had the Antonia Mason file on his desk. Strange business; he wondered if they would ever get to the bottom of it. It did seem that she had some sort of connection to the Blenthorne Inn, but none of it made any sense.

The Blenthorne Inn immediately took his thoughts back to Lizzie Lockwood – or Lizzie Tennyson as she was when he first met her. He was a young constable at the time and had seen her on a couple of occasions before that wild night when he had had to go and tell her that her husband Richard had died in a car accident. He remembered the wind howling with the rain teeming down and dripping off his uniform as he stood outside the back door of the inn. She had opened the door and politely invited him in.

He broke her heart that night.

He watched her as he delivered the news of the accident and the spirit seemed to drain out of her. She looked at him in disbelief, her eyes wide and questioning. Tears started to fall down her cheeks unchecked but she made no sound. She had answered the questions he had asked her clearly and concisely.

As he took her to the hospital he was amazed at her self-control. Her hands were clenched and her knuckles white; her jaw set tight but she made no sound. Now and again she flicked a tear from her face. He had stayed with her at the hospital and had taken her home afterwards. In fact he had been reluctant to leave her; he still remembered Ruby Bumstead ushering him away so that she could put Lizzie to bed.

The accident report found that Richard Tennyson's brakes were faulty, a bit more than the usual amount of wear and tear to be expected in a car of that age but Lizzie explained they had clocked up the miles since they decided to move to the Lake District. They had made lots of trips to and from their home in the south east of England when they were looking for a property and since moving, there had been the inevitable mileage incurred in setting up a new business. The car was due for an MOT a couple of weeks after the accident, in fact Richard had been planning to take it into the garage shortly. Coupled with the conditions on the night in question and his speed at the time of the accident, it was all pretty cut and dried – a silly senseless avoidable accident which had deprived a young lad of his father and a kind and caring lady of her husband.

He had liaised with Lizzie a few times afterwards by phone and made a couple of courtesy calls following the funeral to see that she was okay; she always smiled politely and said she was and finally he had run out of excuses to visit in line with his professional duty. At the time he hadn't really thought about her further, at least that is what he had liked to tell himself.

He got up and went over to the kitchen area to make himself a cup of coffee. The sugar was damp as usual with the odd coffee granule sticking out of it. Well, better for him not to have any. He had nothing to rush home for; no football on the telly tonight; no meal waiting for him; no homework to help the boys with; no he could just stay put to get things clear in his head before tomorrow. He went back to his desk stirring the coffee. He flicked through the file before him.

He next had occasion to see Lizzie after Jim Lockwood, her second husband, had contacted the police as a result of seeing a media appeal for information about Antonia Mason, whose body had been found in the area. He picked up the photograph before him; quite an attractive young lady he thought, though maybe a bit obvious. Jim had a friend called um – he flicked through the file ... George Johnson – Jono to his mates – who in turn knew Antonia – or Toni as she liked to be called. It appeared she was an independent financial adviser and she was planning to see Jim about life insurance.

She had apparently never got in touch with Jim. He didn't think anything more about it and Jono Johnson had assumed she had gone abroad as planned when he did not hear from her, as he knew she had been thinking about it.

Her mother had reported her missing two years before her body was found; although it seemed they had not been close. Her mother was living with a new partner and Antonia did not get on with her step-family. Mrs Mason could not give police a current address for her daughter, only that she was probably living in the north somewhere and she was not quite sure when they had last had contact. It was assumed that she was possibly abroad, although no record of her leaving the country could be found.

She appeared to be self-employed and the company she had been working for on a commission only basis hadn't actively pursued the matter when she failed to turn up for work. She was a bit unreliable and often missed the odd day after partying it seemed. The world of insurance was a pretty transient business at that time. Her landlord had assumed she had done a bunk without paying the rent. He admitted he had collected up her possessions and sold what he could at a car boot sale as recompense. The rest he had given to charity or dumped.

Gary wondered why the media had not shown more interest in the missing person report, as an attractive young lady usually generated quite a bit of publicity. He looked at the date of the report filed by her mother. May 1997 – he checked the internet. Oh yes, the same time as the general election when Rule Britannia was giving way to Cool Britannia, ending eighteen years of government by the previous lot – he smiled ironically – he well remembered the hype heralding what was supposed to be an exciting new era in British politics. The papers were full of it; little else seemed to be newsworthy at the time.

So it appeared that Antonia Mason had just vanished off the planet until her body turned up.

He recalled interviewing Jim Lockwood and subsequently Lizzie. Jim had come across as a straightforward sort of chap with nothing to hide. Gary had no reason to suppose he was lying, although it did seem strange that Toni had planned to see him and then for her remains to finally turn up a few miles away.

It was really the only lead they had. The post mortem was inconclusive and did not give them any clear lines of enquiry to follow. The damage to the skull was conceivably consistent with a fall. Clearly it had come in contact with a hard object or objects; however there were many large hard objects in the form of rocks and boulders on the descent from the top of Hell's Drop to the bottom. The body had apparently been wedged in a gully. The clothing, what was left of it, was bog standard and could be purchased from any high street and the type favoured by walkers. He and a colleague had questioned Jim extensively for several hours. He had the witness statement in front of him. After going over his story several times, Jim had put it to Gary that if he really did have something to hide, would he have actually come forward?

Gary had to concede he had a point. Also what was his motive? It appeared he had never met Toni before and if it was a sexual assault gone wrong, there was certainly no evidence obtained to support that theory; although the body being outside for years hadn't helped their forensic colleagues.

Also there was nothing in Jim's background to suggest he had any proclivity in that direction. He was ex-army with an outstanding service record – Gary had checked with the Ministry of Defence. Jim had been part of small group from his battalion that was ambushed during a reconnoitre operation during the Gulf campaign. He and three others had survived the attack but two of his comrades had been killed outright. Jim it appeared had shielded his wounded officer until help arrived but sadly the lieutenant did not survive his wounds and died some weeks later in hospital in England. Jim himself sustained minor physical injuries.

He noted there had been mental health issues both prior and subsequent to his discharge from military service but never any suggestion of violence. No, there was nothing more they could have done regarding Jim. He turned the page over and looked at Lizzie's witness statement.

He thought back to the day she had come into the interview room. She looked good he thought – not classically beautiful or indeed even pretty but she had something about her, something that just made people respond to her. Oddly, he could still remember what she was wearing – blue jeans with a black cable knit jumper and a long gold necklace covered by a smart black jacket. "Attempting to look effortlessly casual" Cheryl called it when she saw Lizzie a few weeks later. Cheryl suggested that Lizzie probably spent hours and hours desperately trying to achieve the "what this? Oh just something I threw on" look. Somehow Cheryl never took to her; he thought she was being unfair. He was sure that Lizzie was in no way scheming.

Gary remembered he had got Lizzie some tea as he looked again at her witness statement. She had wrapped her hands around the cup and sipped it slowly as it was piping hot. He had asked her about Antonia Mason and whether she had ever had any contact with her. She shook her head and her hair escaped from behind her left ear. She had pushed it back without fuss – he couldn't imagine Lizzie making a fuss about anything.

He tore himself away from the memory and concentrated on the statement before him which confirmed that she had never spoken to Antonia or even seen her; she explained that Jim was expecting to hear from someone called Tony in regard to some insurance advice and they had both assumed it was a man as Jono had not been specific about her gender or when she would ring. When they didn't hear anything, Jim had arranged the life insurance through the bank a few weeks before they got married.

They had both been incredibly surprised to find out that the body found in Hell's Drop was in fact the remains of the person who was due to make contact with Jim. He remembered with a smile that Lizzie had used the word "gobsmacked" and then put her hand over her mouth, wondering if she could say that in a statement.

Obviously she did not know the timescale involved. It could have been that Antonia had visited the area subsequent to Jono suggesting she get in touch with Jim for a totally different reason. However, she was sure that Jim had never had any contact with Antonia, he would have told her. They had no secrets, what possible motive could Jim have for not telling her? He was an open book and furthermore, with his background he above all people knew the precious value of life.

Gary was forced to agree with her. What a lucky man Jim Lockwood was thought Gary ironically as he saw Lizzie to the door.

He discussed the statements with his inspector the following day. Detective Inspector Bob Davis asked if Gary thought it would be worth searching the Blenthorne Inn; he doubted they had enough for a search warrant but if Mr and Mrs Lockwood were happy to co-operate maybe they would agree to a search. DI Davis left it to Gary to decide, it was his call.

On balance he really could not see the point. There were no sightings of Toni in the area and her car was nowhere to be found. No, he was sure the whole thing was just a coincidence. He decided to leave the statements on file, unless or until any further information came to light.

He and a couple of mates went to the Blenthorne Inn for a drink a few days later and got chatting to Maggie Blake the barmaid. He casually asked if she had seen anyone who fitted Antonia Mason's description going back several years. Maggie laughed and said she couldn't recall the faces of the people she had served yesterday let alone years ago. However she had seen the picture on the TV and did not recognise the lady but in view of the number of people who swelled the population at times, that was not surprising. Lizzie had appeared at that point and said that "the boys" could have a drink on the house, which was very obliging of her.

He and Cheryl had enjoyed a lovely meal at the restaurant a couple of weeks later and Lizzie made them feel very special. Cheryl constantly referred to Lizzie as "your girlfriend" when speaking of her to Gary. Whilst she had said it in what he thought was jest, Gary was appalled to think he was potentially so transparent.

He had enjoyed many an evening at the Blenny after that time, either having a drink and bar snack or a formal meal in the restaurant. Many of his colleagues dined there; not regularly as Lockwood's was a bit pricey for anything more than a special occasion, although Lizzie and Jim had given them a great deal on their Christmas parties.

They also did a "friends and family" night once every other month on a Tuesday, extending to almost everyone they knew when dinner was half price so that encouraged the locals. Gary thought it was nice that they were not hard-nosed business types who had forgotten about the people they lived among. Yes, he had a lot of time for Lizzie and Jim too of course.

That made what had happened recently all the more strange and confusing. He had had a call from Lizzie a year or so previously to say she had had an encounter with a young man called Luke Farmer. Luke seemed to think he knew Lizzie from the past – he said he believed she had stolen a car. Luke had tried to blackmail her over this and she had immediately contacted him to ask his advice. He was intrigued at that point.

He had looked Luke Farmer up on the computer and sure enough he had a record as long as your arm as the saying goes. These could mostly be classified as dishonesty offences: burglary, car theft and handling stolen property – nothing violent. He suggested Lizzie should arrange a meeting with Luke and Gary would be present and he could take it from there.

As it turned out the little tosser had scarpered as soon as Gary introduced himself. He had subsequently spoken to the owners of the Fell View Hotel who had said they had dismissed Luke a few days previously as he had not been able to produce valid references and they did not feel he was suitable for the job. He had filed a report, which was also now in front of him, but there the matter ended – until today.

He had received a phone call this afternoon from a Flying Squad team to say that a Luke Farmer had been arrested the previous day for an attempted armed robbery in London. Stupid silly little so-and-so had got mixed up in something that was way out of his league. What the team were really after was information about his associates with a connection to the robbery but he was shit scared – literally the officer told him grimly! He refused to name names and no amount of pressure and persuasion so far had encouraged him to change his mind. He would rather go down for years than squeal as he put it.

The officer went on to say that when Luke realised just how long a stretch he was looking at, he started shouting wildly that he knew something about a suspicious death – a woman by the name of Antonia Mason – remains found about five years ago in Gary's neck of the woods. Luke wanted to barter that information in exchange for a reduced charge. He was saying he would only speak to Gary – could he throw any light on it? Gary thought it was rubbish but he needed to check it out properly and consequently was planning a trip to London the following day.

He closed the files and got up from his chair, picking up his jacket as he did so. He said goodnight to the cleaners who were working round him and left the office. He would see what tomorrow would bring. A wild goose chase, he would put money on it.

*

He arrived in London the following lunchtime having caught an early train from Carlisle to Euston Station and was collected by DC Cathy Sheppard. Having eaten on the train, Gary turned down the offer of food but had a cup of tea prior to going to the interview room to question Luke Farmer.

The room was simply furnished with plain off white walls and no window; there was an air conditioning vent built into the ceiling as well as a camera on the wall. There was a grey metal desk and chairs around it for those present – himself, DC Sheppard and Luke Farmer who had a duty solicitor with him.

Gary made the introductions after the DC had loaded the visual and audio recording equipment. He also gave the date and time.

'Hello Luke – this had better be good,' said Gary as he took the seat on the opposite side of the desk.

'I'm not saying anything until I find out what charges are going to be brought against me. That is the condition for my co-operation.'

'Outside my control I'm afraid,' said Gary grimly as he leaned back in his chair. 'I'm here because you wanted to see me so either give me what you think you've got or stop wasting my time.'

Luke folded his arms and looked away.

'Okay if that's the way you want it; no point me hanging round here, I'll get the next train back to Carlisle. Take care of yourself Luke.' Gary got up, pushed his chair under the desk and walked towards the door. Luke whispered rapidly with his solicitor.

'It's about that woman – that Lockwood woman – the one you were with in Keswick. It's about her,' said Luke quickly in a loud enough voice for Gary to hear as he was about to leave the room.

'What about her?' enquired Gary feigning disinterest as he sauntered back to the desk and pulled out the chair again in order to sit down.

'What did she tell you the day you were with her in Keswick? Did she tell you why I wanted to see her?' asked Luke shoving his hands in his pockets as he leaned back in his chair, balancing it on its back legs.

'How about I ask the questions and you answer them – that's the way it usually works in police interviews,' said Gary as he sat down once more.

'I saw her in Carlisle years ago; she was driving a hatchback and she left it in a car park near the shopping centre about midday on Wednesday 7 August 1996. I was on the lookout for a car of that type if you understand me – and well there she was, getting out of this gold coloured hatchback.'

'Is that it? Sorry Luke, you are telling me you saw a lady who looked like Lizzie Lockwood getting out of a hatchback in a car park in Carlisle on a Wednesday in August nine years ago – have I really come 300 miles to hear that?'

'It wasn't any hatchback; it was the one belonging to that woman whose body was found at that place – what's it – Hell's Leap or Drop or something. I noticed particularly because she left the keys in the ignition and the door unlocked – I thought it was odd at the time but looking back afterwards it seemed to me that she obviously wanted somebody to steal it. Now you need to ask yourself Detective Sergeant, just what was she doing dumping a car belonging to a dead woman in a car park miles from her home?' Luke looked very pleased with himself as he leaned forward once more, allowing the chair to regain its stable four-legged position.

'How can you be so specific regarding the date – the remains found in Hell's Drop weren't discovered until several years after that, so Antonia Mason might not even have been dead at the time,' said Gary, rather confused by what he was hearing.

'I can be specific because my sister got married the weekend after and there were a newish pair of white shoes in the boot of the car which I gave to her; she preferred them to the ones she had bought and wore them for her wedding. I also remembered the number plate because in my profession it pays to keep track of that sort of thing. So I am telling you; Lizzie Lockwood drove the dead woman's car to Carlisle on the date I said.'

'So you were stealing cars to order, is that what you are telling me Luke; that is your "profession" is it?'

Luke didn't answer; he just continued to look smug.

'Come on Detective, I have kept my part of the bargain; what are you going to do for me?'

Gary did not respond; he silently studied Luke as he sat before him, his face expressionless.

'If you don't believe me, then ask yourself this; why didn't you or anyone else try to find me and charge me with attempted blackmail eh? It's a pretty serious offence I think isn't it? I will tell you my guess shall I? She asked you not to pursue it didn't she – probably said no harm done and not to make a fuss – am I right?'

Gary still said nothing. In fact Luke was completely correct – Lizzie had asked him not to take it any further. He had thought at the time it was because she was just a thoroughly decent lady who did not want to make trouble for others but what if, what if – there was another reason? What if there was some truth in what Luke had told him?

'I will look into what you have told me Luke – thank you for volunteering this information. Goodbye and good luck; I think you may need it.'

'What about me? Are you going to speak up for me?'

Gary got up and left the room with Luke shouting after him.

Before leaving he assured the DCI in charge that Luke had been of help but it was entirely up to them if they took that into account with regard his involvement in their case.

Gary got the first train he could from Euston to Carlisle. His thoughts were in turmoil. It sounded incredible but what had Luke got to gain from lying about it? Taken on its own it maybe could be dismissed as the product of a fertile imagination but put together with the fact that Jim Lockwood had openly admitted to having a connection with the dead woman, however tenuous, it was certainly something that he would at least need to speak to Lizzie about.

He would give her a ring and suggest they have a chat tomorrow; either at the station or maybe just informally to start with at the Blenny. He also wondered if he should apply for a search warrant; maybe not make it too formal, after all the word of someone like Luke Farmer should probably be taken with a pinch of salt. Most likely there was a simple explanation or maybe Luke was just making mischief – he was in a hole after all – either way, he would chat with Lizzie and get this all sorted out. In fact if he asked her, he was sure Lizzie would just tell him to look where he wanted!

The problem was he just could not shake the idea that there was possibly more to it than that.

He fell asleep finally on the rather uncomfortable train seat and woke with a start. He felt very chilly by the time he reached his stop and got off the train.

He collected his car and drove home. His dark flat was as usual completely unwelcoming. He took off his jacket and found a jumper to put on as he was still chilled to the bone. He looked in the freezer compartment for a meal-for-one which he removed from its sleeve and put in the microwave after piercing the plastic lid. He found a cold beer in the fridge and contemplated how he was going to deal with the interview tomorrow. In the end after a lot of thought, he decided it would be best to play it by ear. The microwave pinged and he put the disposable tray onto a plate and took both his meal and beer through to the lounge area on a tray.

He switched on the television and sat on the sofa. An hour later he did not remember eating his food or what he had watched.

He got up and made his way wearily towards the bedroom; tomorrow was probably going to be a very difficult day he thought apprehensively.

The following morning he went to the office and spoke to his inspector. They discussed all that had transpired in London and agreed an action plan. Gary would speak to Lizzie informally at home and see what that would elicit – if anything. If he was satisfied with what she told him then they would leave the matter on file but if he had anything at all to go on, an active investigation would follow.

He found her number and rang Lizzie with no sense of foreboding regarding what the day ahead had in store for him.

Chapter 11

Lizzie – 2005

Lizzie put the phone down. Gary Carmichael was coming to see her later that morning. He was rather evasive with regard the reason over the phone, in fact he sounded a little on edge. She wondered what could be wrong; she hoped it was nothing to do with Luke Farmer. Things had been quiet on that front since the day in Keswick when she had confronted him with Gary in tow – but no, that was ages ago – she really did need to learn to relax! He probably wanted to see her about something completely different – a discount on a group booking at the restaurant maybe. Yes it would be something like that.

She went upstairs to freshen up. A bit more make up wouldn't go amiss. She also changed out of her old jeans and put on some that were a bit more flattering. She brushed her hair and sprayed perfume around her.

She had just taken delivery of a parcel – she never could resist a catalogue clothes sale – and had been trying to unwrap it however it was proving resistant to all her attempts. She was rummaging in the top drawer of her desk for some scissors when she heard what she thought was Gary's car draw up in the car park. She found the scissors, placed them on the desk and was waiting at the back door with a smile on her face as he walked towards her.

'Morning Gary; lovely day,' she said with a bright smile.

'Yes indeed Lizzie, lovely,' replied Gary in what Lizzie thought was a rather pensive way. He clearly had something on his mind she thought.

'You look very sombre; what's wrong?' she asked with a certain amount of trepidation.

'Let's go in and sit down shall we – there is something I need to talk to you about.'

'Well that not only sounds serious but a bit scary! Do you want some tea or coffee?' Lizzie asked, trying to remain upbeat.

'No thank you, not at the moment anyway. The thing is Lizzie ... we have known each other a long time haven't we? I'll come straight to the point, it involves Luke Farmer.'

They sat down in the office on chairs facing each other.

'Oh my goodness that's a name from the past – so he has been caught has he – what has he done this time? I know you said he would probably continue to commit offences,' said Lizzie her thoughts racing as she tried to look calm and collected.

'Quite right – only this time he's got way in over his head. He's been arrested by the police in London for his involvement in an armed robbery on a jewellers' shop. Daft little so-and-so managed to attract the attention of the owner's dog, which was kept on the premises as more of a deterrent than anything else. The robbery was foiled by the courageous owner and the shopkeeper next door who ran to his aid. The other robbers took off but wouldn't you know it, poor old Luke ended up with his left leg in the dog's mouth.'

'So caught in the act then,' said Lizzie forcing a smile.

'Indeed he was. The thing is Lizzie he wouldn't give us any information on his associates as he is considerably more afraid of reprisals from them than anything we can throw at him.'

'I see; so what exactly is your involvement? You said London; a bit outside your patch surely?'

'Yes absolutely. Basically I had a call the day before yesterday from the team there to ask if I would like to go down as Luke was saying he had some information which he would only give to me. So I spent part of yesterday interviewing him.'

'Go on,' said Lizzie swallowing as she tried to quell the alarm mounting inside her.

'Fundamentally Luke is hoping to save his own skin and thought if he gave me certain information it would bode well for him with regard the charges to be brought against him. I told him I had no influence over that, but would listen to what he had to say,' said Gary shifting slightly in his chair.

Lizzie remained silent, her arms folded in her lap and her face set in a small smile which did not reach her eyes.

'You will remember that day in Keswick I'm sure when you suggested he was trying to blackmail you with regards a stolen car? It really didn't seem to make any sense at the time but he has now suggested there was a bit more to it than that. He told me the car in question was a hatchback. Subsequently he realised it was the car registered to Antonia Mason.'

'And just how does that involve me exactly?' interrupted Lizzie.

'Well, the thing is Luke is insisting he saw you leave the car in a car park in Carlisle the first Wednesday in August 1996. I know it sounds crazy, but that is what he has told me. He can apparently be specific as to the date. So I suppose my question to you is – is there any truth at all in what he is saying?'

'None whatsoever,' said Lizzie looking him straight in the eye.

'Why do you think he has said it then?' asked Gary his head slightly on one side as he looked at Lizzie enquiringly.

'Gary, as you said at the beginning, we have known each other a long time, presumably in that time you have formed an opinion as to my character and disposition. You told me yourself Luke Farmer has a long criminal record – so do you really think there could be a grain of truth in the word of a convicted lawbreaker? You have met him, he can be quite charming and articulate – he would probably say anything for effect. He certainly took my friends Robin and Mark who run the hotel in the village for a ride. So my question to you is: how on earth could you take seriously anything he has told you? He must be quite used to spinning a yarn to get out of a tight spot. Are you really going to take his word over mine? Even if you do, what evidence do you have? A description of a woman who looks like me leaving a car in a car park in Carlisle, what is it nine years ago? Please Gary! This is quite unbelievable.'

'You are quite correct; I have no evidence. No blanket CCTV coverage in city centres in those days of course – that would have helped us considerably. We could have sorted it out one way or the other.'

Lizzie thought about using the bus ticket alibi – she had hung on to those lest she was asked about Carlisle at the time, however that would now look strange to have kept bus tickets for nine years just in case she was asked about that day, so she decided against it. In fact so confident was she after Naomi's death, she wasn't quite sure she still had them; she had made a cursory search to no avail after Luke had tried to blackmail her – and now here was the bloody car causing her problems again.

'I do go to Carlisle quite often of course; and I park in a variety of car parks, depending on where I need to go and where I can find a space. So he may well have seen me in the area if he used to hang around the place waiting for an opportunity to take a vehicle. I have no idea if I was in Carlisle that day or not, so it is quite possible that he did see me, but not connected with the vehicle in question.' Lizzie smiled as she stood up.

Gary did not move.

'Lizzie, would you mind if I had a look round while I am here?' asked Gary leaning forward in his chair.

'Gary! What on earth are you looking for? Do you think I have a blood stained axe under the stairs? Or maybe I have Antonia's shoes stashed in a cupboard?' Lizzie started pacing the room.

Gary looked up with a start

'Why did you mention her shoes Lizzie?'

Hell thought Lizzie. The damned shoes – now she remembered; she had put them in the boot of the hatchback before she took it to Carlisle as she didn't think they would burn in the bonfire. She stood still and looked at him wide eyed.

'It was just a figure of speech, no more – I could have said her handbag or her coat, however I said her shoes.'

'Yes but you did actually say "shoes" rather than anything else. Why did you think of shoes first? The reason I ask is that Luke said that he could pinpoint the day with accuracy because he found a nearly new pair of white shoes in the boot of the hatchback and gave them to his sister who in turn chose to wear them for her wedding the following weekend.'

'No, there was no particular reason that I said "shoes" first. I thought we were having a conversation; I didn't realise it was a grilling with every word I uttered being scrutinised and turned against me. Honestly Gary, I am not really sure I know you at all. Do you really think I could be involved in a suspicious death?'

'The truth is Lizzie I don't think you could. There is only one reason that you might be,' he paused and looked at her closely, 'and that is to protect Jim,' he said very quietly.

Lizzie felt herself tense all over. No, not Jim, Gary couldn't possibly think he was involved.

'He admitted at the time that Antonia could be in the area to see him,' said Gary evenly as he looked closely at Lizzie.

'And why would he do that if he had murdered her? This is madness, I won't listen to any more of it – Gary please leave now. Arrest me or leave.' Lizzie was standing squarely in front of Gary breathing hard and struggling to get enough air into her lungs to speak.

'Wow – slow down Lizzie, no one said anything about arrest did they. Now please sit down. Hypothetically, if Jim had thought he had been seen with Antonia then possibly he may have decided it would be a good idea to mention his involvement however tenuous, before we made the connection ourselves.'

'But he had no "involvement" as you put it. He had never met the woman!' Lizzie's voice was getting higher and higher as she tried in vain to control her temper and keep her breathing regular. She felt the temporal vein on the right side of her forehead start to throb.

She really hadn't thought of this angle. The idea that Jim could be suspected of her crime was unthinkable. She ran her hands through her hair, tugging at it as she did so.

'Please Lizzie sit down; can you be absolutely sure he had never met Antonia? I am not suggesting that Jim murdered her; it's conceivable that they argued and there was some sort of accident. He could have then panicked and asked you to help him – is that possible Lizzie? Did you help Jim dispose of her body or did you just drive the car to Carlisle afterwards?'

'No absolutely not. Why would he meet her and argue with her – it doesn't make any sense.'

'I'm not sure how to put this delicately, but she was an attractive young lady – do you think there is any possibility that they could have been having an affair? He tried to end it, she got angry, tempers flared or maybe she tried to end it and somehow she …'

'I really don't believe I am hearing this Gary – Jim have an affair; that is about as crazy as suggesting I would have one!'

How ironic this was thought Lizzie – she had believed that Antonia was Sarah and was convinced she would lose Jim and now Gary thought he was having an affair with Antonia.

'You just wait until Jim gets home Gary – he will tell you; this is wrong, it's all wrong. You could not be more misguided if you tried.' Lizzie was panting for breath.

'Actually Jim won't be home for a while. My boss rang him earlier; he has voluntarily attended the police station and is being questioned as we speak. I had a message just before I arrived here to say Jim was happy for us to take a look round. So we will get on with that now if that's okay with you.'

'No, it is not okay with me – I think you will find it is my name above the door as licensee so if you want to look round you obtain a search warrant. You won't find anything as there is nothing to find but that is not the point. You have stretched our friendship to the limit and I have no obligation to co-operate with you any further.'

'Okay if that is how you feel – I think maybe we had better go off to the station now Lizzie, we can continue this a bit more formally. I really hope that we can sort it out.'

Who did he think he was? Suggesting Jim would have an affair; accusing her of being an accomplice to murder. Jim would never hurt anyone; but how could she make him see that without incriminating herself? Jim would be at the police station now being interrogated – how would his mental state hold up to that – worse still, would he confess to something he had not done to make the questions stop?

Lizzie was in a state of blind panic. She believed she had covered her tracks sufficiently but all she had actually done was throw suspicion onto Jim.

'Come on love, get your coat if you want one and we can be off,' said Gary in what Lizzie thought was a very patronising way as he rose from the chair.

Lizzie could see flashes in front of her eyes; big black spots dancing before her. She walked over to the desk and slowly picked up the scissors.

She needed to end this situation; she had to have some room so that she could think of the best thing to do. Gary was close behind her, invading her personal space. Worse still he had called her "love". How she hated that – so denigrating. She could feel the molten lava bubbling up inside her again.

'That's right, it won't take long I'm sure,' said Gary as he attempted to steer her towards the door as if she were a small child.

That was the final straw; he had gone too far.

'Let go of me!' she yelled furiously as she spun round and without thinking of the consequences, thrust the scissors point first into his chest. They appeared to embed themselves very easily she thought as his shirt started to turn dark red and a metallic smell invaded her nostrils.

Lizzie stepped back; at first she just stared at Gary and then looked at her hands, blood seeping through her fingers.

Gary looked down in disbelief at the scissors rooted in his chest. He let out a small moan and swayed towards a chair. Lizzie sprang forward and he put out his hands in an attempt to try to fend her off.

'Oh Gary, what have I done?' Lizzie looked at him in horror as she helped him into a chair.

'Please forgive me – I don't know what came over me. I will get help.' Lizzie went to the phone and picking up the handset, rang the emergency services. As she did so Maggie came through from the bar and stared at the scene before her.

'It's okay Maggie, there has been a bit of an accident; I have rung the police and for an ambulance,' said Lizzie as she pressed tissues from the box on the desk to Gary's chest around where the scissors were embedded in an attempt to stop the bleeding.

Gary was looking grey and sweating, his breathing increasingly laboured. Maggie clutched the door for support and appeared paralysed with fear. The ambulance seemed to take ages but in reality it was no more than a few minutes, with the police following shortly behind. Lizzie kept the pressure on Gary's chest until the paramedic intervened and asked her to step away.

Lizzie told the attending police officers that she had stabbed Gary with the scissors and was immediately arrested. She asked if she could wash her hands before she left and was not allowed to do so, a police officer put plastic bags over them instead. She collected her jacket and walked quietly to the police car with an officer on either side of her.

No one spoke during the journey. Lizzie stared out of the car window in a daze. She was taken to Keswick Police Station where she was charged with wounding a police officer in the execution of his duty and causing grievous bodily harm with intent.

She had had time to think during the journey and decided there was really only one thing she could do – she had to spare Jim from anymore interrogation. She declared she wished to make a statement in regard to the death of Antonia Mason.

She had no choice; she had to protect Jim.

She was transferred to the main police station in Carlisle and was placed in an interview room with an officer in attendance until Inspector Davis arrived to interview her. She was shaking excessively and the police duty doctor was called to check she was fit to be interviewed.

It was decided she would be remanded in custody overnight and be interviewed the following day.

The next day, Friday, 1 July 2005, Elizabeth Louise Lockwood confessed to causing the death of Antonia Frances Mason aged thirty-two from Newcastle and was charged with the voluntary manslaughter on or around 7 August 1996. She was also charged with the concealment of evidence and disposal of a body.

She was remanded in custody for sentencing, having waived the right to a trial by jury under common law.

Lizzie's world was crumbling around her and she was powerless to stop it. What had happened to the bright optimistic young woman who had come to live in the Lake District with her family all those years ago?

How had she come to this and what would the future hold for her now?

Chapter 12

Judgement Day 2006

Lizzie was waiting to be called before the judge for sentencing and was feeling nervous. Events had moved swiftly since her arrest.

She was amazed to discover that she was to face no charges in connection with the stabbing of Gary Carmichael.

Once recovered sufficiently from his right sided pneumothorax, Gary had made a statement to the effect that Lizzie had picked up the scissors and believing she intended to harm herself, he attempted to wrestle them from her. During the ensuing struggle, he was accidentally stabbed in the chest. His actions were foolish and as he had placed himself in a dangerous situation, no blame could be attached to her. He had known Lizzie for a long time and to suggest there was any malicious intent would be inconceivable.

Alex had rung their solicitor in Keswick who had put them in touch with a lawyer specialising in criminal law. When Lizzie first met Nicola Hallam she felt a chill run down her spine. Nicola was in her early thirties, tall and slim with long blonde hair and she was wearing a smart dark trouser suit and white blouse. She looked uncannily like Antonia Mason – not a good omen. However, when she spoke the similarity ended. Nicola was pleasant, calm and highly articulate. Lizzie thought that those qualities were probably prerequisites for solicitors.

Nicola was rather dismayed that Lizzie had confessed without legal representation and waived her right to a trial by jury; however she said it could play in their favour. She would stress the fact that Lizzie was so overcome with remorse that she needed to get her crimes off her chest. It would be up to the judge to pass sentence, so they needed to look at presenting the facts in as favourable a light as possible.

Nicola asked Lizzie to talk her through what had happened. They were sitting in an interview room in the police station. Nicola had a pad and pen in front of her on the table and was making notes as Lizzie talked.

Lizzie had by now had plenty of time to embellish and ameliorate her version of events. Obviously she did not want to mention mistaken identity. She explained that Antonia had knocked on the door when the pub was closed. She had seemed in an excitable state and Lizzie had allowed her in as she was worried about her. Antonia had started asking questions about Jim without explaining who she was, other than that she knew him through a mutual friend. Lizzie was very protective of Jim due to his history of PTSD and for this reason did not want to discuss him with someone she didn't know. Antonia became very loud and quite verbally aggressive. Lizzie wondered if she was under the influence of some type of recreational drug.

Unfortunately Lizzie had allowed herself to be provoked by Antonia when she made some comments about Jim's past, suggesting that he would never recover from his wartime experiences. When Lizzie became upset, Antonia laughed at her.

Lizzie told Nicola of something her vicar had once said during a sermon: "sticks and stones can break your bones, but words can break your heart" those words, a variation on the well-known quote, had seemed pertinent at that particular moment and Lizzie had picked up the nearest thing to hand and hurled it at Antonia.

She had not really meant to hit her, just throw something in her general direction to scare her a bit and make her stop laughing. Regrettably she had used more force than she intended and it caught Antonia on the temple and she fell heavily, hitting her head on the edge of the desk as she went down.

When Lizzie realised Antonia was dead she most certainly should have contacted the police; however, in a fit of madness she did not do so. She concealed the body and subsequently disposed of it by taking it to Hell's Drop where she tipped it over the edge.

Lizzie thought that sounded believable and didn't contradict anything she had previously told the police prior to being charged. She looked up through her fringe at Nicola in a sad and dejected way.

Nicola said she thought they had a good case for provocation due to temporary loss of self-control and she would be in contact with the barrister to arrange a meeting between the three of them. She particularly liked the "sticks and stones" reference and made a mental note to use that in the future; it was possible another defendant could benefit from such a thought-provoking remark, juries loved things like that.

After her confession Lizzie had been placed on remand, having made no application for bail and subsequent meetings between her and the defence team were held at the prison.

Lizzie's barrister was a middle aged lady by the name of Helen Colman. She was small and quite round and wearing a pale pink blouse that Lizzie thought looked a bit tight as it kept riding up every time she moved and she had to keep tugging it down into place. She had neat closely cropped grey hair. Her manner was reassuring and confident. Her glasses were perched on the end of her nose and she was either peering over the top or lifting up her chin so that she could actually see through them. She agreed with Nicola that their defence was appropriate in the circumstances and she would speak to the Crown Prosecution Service.

'What a shame you actually dumped the body – we might have got you five years if you had owned up straight away. You would have been out in two. The Judge won't like the fact you flung it off a cliff. You will get a few years added on for that I'm afraid.'

'Yes I know I behaved shamefully; I can never forgive myself,' said Lizzie gravely. 'At least I am only being charged in connection with the death of Antonia, I am not facing prosecution for wounding a police officer. He has very kindly spoken up for me.'

'Yes, well we don't want to complicate matters by bringing that up do we? We don't want the Judge to think you make a habit of lunging at people with anything to hand. So don't mention it to anyone,' Helen warned sternly. 'In fact I don't need to call you at all. I will make the necessary plea regarding mitigating circumstances in the pre-sentencing report.' She sniffed as she pushed her glasses up her nose a bit, only for them to drop down to their original position within a few seconds.

Lizzie randomly thought the sniffing sounded a bit like her mother and wondered if she dared to suggest that Helen might have more luck with her glasses if she applied some more translucent powder to her face to counteract the rather greasy appearance of her foundation preparation. On balance, it was probably best not to mention it.

Lizzie's first court appearance had been a brief one where she just had to enter her plea. The judge had then adjourned the case for the pre-sentencing report to be prepared and scrutinised.

That morning Lizzie had been driven to the Crown Court in Carlisle, locked into a small compartment inside a security van. She was greatly relieved to get out and stretch her legs. She was taken into court via a back entrance by a guard to whom she was handcuffed. She was wearing her formal black dress with a matching jacket. Her hair was loose and she had used a minimum of makeup.

She was led up into the dock from the holding area downstairs. She looked around her as she got her bearings. She gripped the bar in front of her. As she had noticed on her first visit, the court was windowless with a predominance of wood. The benches where the jury would normally be sitting were empty. The judge sat in his high backed chair on a raised dais facing the court. He looked a bit overweight Lizzie thought absentmindedly.

She glanced up to the public gallery. There was Alex sitting with Faye, Bert, Ruby and Maggie. Maggie waved slightly and Lizzie smiled up at her so that Maggie could see that she was okay. Robin was there also smiling down at her.

Jim was not among those present but Lizzie thought charitably maybe he had decided to stay behind and run the pub as he probably felt it would be too upsetting for her to see him. She was told to sit down by a court official and the guard in attendance sat next to her.

The proceedings started and Lizzie found she was not really listening; it all seemed surreal, like it was happening to someone else. However she forced herself back to the present as her defence counsel got to her feet.

Helen Colman pushed her glasses up her nose and spoke eloquently for several minutes and the judge made notes as she put the case before him. She spoke of the mitigating circumstances which led Elizabeth Lockwood to commit the crime of manslaughter due to provocation leading to a temporary loss of self-control. She went on to talk about Lizzie's subsequent behaviour and emphasised how completely out of character it had been and something for which Lizzie was and would continue to be eternally sorry.

The judge decided he had enough to think about for an hour or two and adjourned the proceedings for lunch.

When he came back he sat down heavily and Lizzie thought he looked a little flushed. She wondered vaguely about his blood pressure for a second or two and was then told to stand while he delivered his speech and pronounce her sentence.

He said he had taken Antonia Mason's personality into account with the personal testimony of George "Jono" Johnson who had known the deceased for some years. He gave a statement to the effect that Antonia Mason could be very pleasant but also had a volatile side to her nature and at times allowed herself to be easily provoked. He highlighted an instance where he had witnessed her getting into a fight with a girl in a night club over an alleged spilt drink. She was also in the habit of taking cannabis and occasionally cocaine.

The judge said he had sympathy for Elizabeth Lockwood and took into account her lack of any previous convictions. It counted in her favour that she had confessed, albeit belatedly, without the need of a trial by jury, thereby saving the taxpayer a vast sum. He accepted that she had acted on impulse and there was no indication of any premeditation. He then spoke of the psychiatric report commissioned by the defence and accepted by the prosecution.

The judge also commented on the number of people who had given character references for Elizabeth Lockwood. He selected a few to read as representative of the whole and commended her on her good works; particularly he noted her devotion to an elderly neighbour with whom she had no previous connection.

However conversely, once Elizabeth Lockwood had regained her self-control, she wilfully concealed evidence by disposing of the body of Antonia Mason, thereby denying her the dignity of being laid to rest. This was a very grave offence and in turn, would aggravate her sentence.

Elizabeth Louise Lockwood was given a custodial sentence of ten years which she would serve in a Category D prison. She would be eligible for release on temporary licence after a portion of her sentence had been served, at the discretion of the parole board.

Lizzie was shaking slightly as she was taken away to start her sentence. She looked up to the gallery as she was led from the dock and saw that Faye had her arm around Alex who appeared to be very upset, his head was down and his shoulders were shaking. Maggie was wiping her eyes and Ruby was talking quietly to her. Robin just looked at Lizzie and smiled reassuringly, nodding slightly.

Lizzie was taken directly to the prison where she had been held on remand and realised sadly that this was to be her home for the foreseeable future. In a strange way she felt relieved that her crimes were no longer secret, she need never again look over her shoulder wondering if she had given herself away and waiting for the next blackmail attempt.

So there she was Lizzie Lockwood: wife, mother, businesswoman, philanthropist, convicted criminal, prisoner.

When she went to bed in her cell she could hear the eerie echoing sounds of the prison bedding down for the night. She pulled the covers tightly around her shoulders and felt more alone than at any other time in her life, with only shadows from the past for company.

Chapter 13

Alex – 2009

Alex Tennyson was taking a break between finishing the lunchtime covers and starting the evening preparations in the restaurant. He had just made himself a cup of tea and was sitting in the rest area, idly flicking through a newspaper. Carl had gone over to the pub to see Maggie.

Alex had been working full time under chef de cuisine Carl Blake for a few years now and felt that he was learning his craft well. Carl was a good teacher who encouraged Alex to experiment and extend his skill set. He had started as a part time kitchen assistant when he was at college and had worked his way up and was now Carl's sous chef.

Prior to that he had unofficially helped his mother in the kitchen of the Blenny for as long as he could remember, probably going back to when his father had been killed in the car accident.

He still remembered that day vividly and supposed he always would. It had been life changing for both him and his mother. He knew nothing about it until the morning after when Ruby Bumstead had woken him up instead of Lizzie.

His mother had the unfortunate habit of noisily entering his room to draw back his curtains with a flourish and calling out "rise and shine" in a completely unnecessary and overly cheerful manner. There was nothing to be so happy about first thing in the morning. For some reason she found it appropriate to get him up at an ungodly hour, as she decreed it was obligatory to shower or bathe on a daily basis, clean his teeth, have breakfast, comb his hair and "make sure everything is ready for school".

As any boy over the age of five can confirm, all that is needed is a ten minute warning prior to leaving the house. Too much bathing serves no purpose and what is the point of a comb when running one's fingers through the hair creates the same effect? He cleaned his teeth at night and didn't eat anything afterwards so that was another unnecessary and time consuming exercise. Just pulling on the school uniform and leaving the house really should be accomplished in well under five minutes, so that left enough time to grab some food on the way out of the door.

However on the day in question there was no happy cheerful swishing of his curtains. Ruby had just sat on the edge of his bed and touched him gently on the shoulder. When he looked up with a start she told him there had been an accident and his mother was in her room and he should go through and see her. She said maybe it would be best if he didn't go to school that day and she would ring them to explain.

When he found out the awful truth he was shattered. His father had been so full of life, ideas burst out of him: he was energetic, enigmatic, charming, happy and funny – the adjectives were endless. Undoubtedly the best dad anyone could wish for. He had been the reason they had moved here. Alex well recalled the arguing prior to them coming. His mother had been so against the idea but in the end she had agreed and they had moved away from everything he had ever known. He remembered the day they had first seen the Blenny; she had squeezed his hand so tightly when they were looking round that he could sense how much she hated it.

However once they were here they both agreed it wasn't so bad. He had made new friends and they seemed fascinated by the fact that he lived above a pub. His mother made such an effort to help him integrate. She invited his classmates for tea, arranged treasure hunts in the garden, made barbeques and invited some parents as well. The beer and wine flowed among the adults and he found himself gaining in popularity very quickly. The invites were returned and he remembered going to parties and to friends' houses to play. He was picked for the school football and rugby teams which again added to his acceptance and status. He had lifts to school when his mother was tied up and his life was generally pretty good. Then it all changed when his dad died.

For a while afterwards he did not know if they would stay in Blenthorne. However he and his mother had had a long chat; she told him whether they stayed or left was a joint decision and she would take on board his opinion and wishes.

As it was, they made a pact to stay, help each other and pull together. He knew they could not have managed alone, Bert, Ruby and Maggie had become their family. Many a night Ruby had put him to bed and asked him if he was too big for a cuddle. He usually insisted he was far too big but occasionally succumbing to the feeling of safety that being enveloped in those warm loving arms gave him. Just when it seemed everything had settled down, Bert had his heart attack.

Again his world somersaulted but then as if by magic, Jim had appeared. For many years he had thought that was a good thing; but now he wasn't so sure. If Jim had never entered their lives, his mother would not have fallen so deeply in love and events would not have turned out as they did.

The decision Jim had just made was going to devastate her.

He and Jim got on extremely well. Their relationship wasn't forced or strained, they got to know each other quite quickly and within a few weeks a mutual respect and liking had developed.

Jim was completely different to his dad Richard. Whereas his dad liked to be larger than life and turn on the charm, Jim wasn't enigmatic or brash, he was quiet, trustworthy and steady and he also had an honesty about him that was reassuring and comforting.

Jim often did the school run or collected him from his sports activities if his mum was busy. They always chatted in the car and on one occasion Alex had asked Jim if he would think about helping out with some of the activities he was involved with, as the clubs he attended were always short of volunteers. Jim had been really pleased to be asked and being quite athletic himself, loved to get involved in football and rugby training as well as officiating. His performances on the cricket pitch though should be glossed over rapidly! Alex vividly remembered a particular "dads and lads" match that had seen a window in a nearby house shattered as finally Jim connected with the ball instead of swishing wildly and hitting fresh air.

Alex sighed. They had been happy times. Carl had suggested on several occasions that maybe he would like to see a bit more of the world than the confines of the small area in which he lived and worked. However, he was so enmeshed in local life, he really had no ambitions in that direction; things might have been different if he hadn't got together with Faye. She wanted them to be near their families so there was no reason to fly further afield. They did like to holiday abroad during the winter school half-term break and particularly enjoyed skiing in Val d'Isère. During the summer holidays they spent a week in the Algarve or sometimes Spain, to see his paternal grandparents and aunt however, after recharging their batteries they were both always ready to return to the normality and security of home.

He had got involved with the local volunteer fell rescue team at Jim's behest. He wasn't sure he had the right skills but he was always eager to help out with fundraising. Faye had also got him involved in raising money for the primary school in Rowendale.

He had been working at the restaurant the day his mother had been arrested. The first thing he knew about it was when Maggie had come bursting through the door and flung herself sobbing into Carl's arms. Carl was grappling with a squid at the time. The events in the back office of the Blenny had all came tumbling out and Carl had made Maggie sit down and tell them what on earth she was talking about.

If she had been thinking straight, Alex was sure she would not have said so much in front of him. As it was, she told them that his mother had stabbed DS Gary Carmichael with a pair of scissors – it made no sense. The ambulance had taken Gary to hospital and police had taken her away. Maggie didn't know what had led to the stabbing but she had heard Lizzie shouting at Gary from the bar where she was setting up.

Alex could not believe what he was hearing, he had tried to ring Jim but his phone was switched off. He subsequently found out that Jim was at the police station already and being interviewed about the death of Antonia Mason, the woman who had been found at the bottom of Hell's Drop.

Alex was in a state of shock. Cue Ruby Bumstead! Alex had no idea how she had heard but assumed that Maggie had rung her mother. In she came, with her sleeves rolled up telling him it would all be sorted out in no time and he must not worry as she was always there. Indeed she was and how he needed her.

What happened next was almost unbelievable. His mother had admitted to the manslaughter of Antonia Mason and the disposal of her body. She was subsequently incarcerated. Alex was in a state of bewilderment and disorientation.

As well as Ruby, his steadying rock, he also had the support of Faye and her family. They had met originally at school. Faye was three years older than Alex but her younger brother Owen was in his year, so inevitably they had seen each other quite a lot when they were growing up. Apparently when they were children, she thought of him as a bit of a nuisance but they became friends when he was older.

She went off to university and he didn't think she would return to the area after she graduated. However she got a job locally, teaching in the reception class at the primary school in Rowendale and moved back in with her parents. He was based at home doing his catering course and they started seeing each other. Things had developed from there; after a while they rented a cottage on the outskirts of the village and they subsequently moved into Naomi Watts' cottage and paid his mother a peppercorn rent for the privilege.

Over the last three and a half years he had visited his mother regularly in prison and still she would not really tell him what had happened or why. She just said it was a "situation that got out of hand and she had not dealt with it very well" – that was the understatement of all time!

He had sat through the court case but it was all a muddle in his head, he could not really remember much about it. He recalled breaking down when his mother was sentenced and Faye having to try to comfort him.

He wanted to think it had been a tragic accident but if so why had his mother disposed of the body; if she did dispose of it? If it wasn't her then there would be only two people in the world that she would lie to protect. He was one and Jim was the other.

Jim had found the whole situation unbelievably traumatic. Alex had hoped they would naturally help each other through the difficult time they were facing but Jim seemed to retreat into his shell.

His mood was very low most of the time and it was not helped by people going to the pub and constantly asking about Lizzie. Jim started seeing a counsellor again and tried to carry on as normal but it didn't seem that his heart was in it. He had found it difficult to visit the prison and Alex could not really get him to open up on the subject. Alex believed he had only been to see Lizzie a couple of times.

Alex knew that a lot of people, the police included, thought his mother had taken the blame for something she may not be fully responsible for. He also knew that Gary Carmichael had spoken to Jim before his mother was sentenced.

Alex had tried to question Jim about the conversation but initially he had not been willing to divulge what had been said. In the end Jim admitted that Gary Carmichael had asked him again if he knew more than he was letting on regarding the death of Antonia Mason. Jim swore to Alex that he didn't. That had to be good enough for him as he trusted Jim. He could not believe that Jim would let his mother take the blame for a crime he had committed – although just occasionally he did have a few doubts.

Jim had begun to be absent for days at a time, more so recently and did not always say where he had been upon his return. Maggie had told Jim she needed help if he was not going to be around as Bert was getting to the point he could not do much at all and was due to have a coronary artery bypass graft soon. Jim had told Maggie to hire what staff she needed, so with the help of both Carl and him, she had done so.

Then yesterday, Jim had dropped the bombshell that he was leaving Blenthorne.

He had asked Alex for a chat and had sat quietly with him in the office. He said he was happy to keep his stake in the restaurant so there were no financial worries on that score for the time being. He had apparently already spoken to Robin and Mark about the hotel and all was sorted there.

He told Alex he had tried to rationalise what Lizzie had done and why, but he couldn't get his head round the events of that fateful day. His counsellor had agreed that he needed to get away from the situation, at least in the short term, as his mental health was not improving.

He asked Alex if, looking back, he had noticed any difference in his mother when they had returned home from their camping trip at that time of the incident.

There was nothing that Alex could specifically remember other than that she had painted the office. She had seemed very excited to see them, but maybe in retrospect it could be argued that her anxiety levels were heightened. What he had thought was excitement may have actually been an adrenaline-infused high as a result of what she had just done.

Jim said the fact that she had managed to live with her conscience for nine years before confessing, showed she had a side to her character that he could not understand or accept.

He felt that everything they had achieved together since that time, including their marriage, had been built on a lie. However he wanted Alex to know that their relationship was the one thing in his life that he hoped would be permanent. He wanted them to stay in touch no matter what the future held.

Jim told Alex he believed that the people of the village treated him differently after Lizzie's arrest. He felt he no longer fitted in. Conversations stopped when he appeared. He knew a lot of their neighbours continued to support them because of their affection for Bert, Maggie and Alex himself. He also thought many tourists came to see the place which had become notorious for being associated with a murder.

'It was not murder Jim, you know that; it was manslaughter,' said Alex, defending his mother quickly.

'Well it resulted in the death of a young woman who would otherwise have been alive if she had not come in contact with your mother,' said Jim with more force in his voice than Alex had ever heard him use.

To be fair he was pretty annoyed when he found Alex had taken some ecstasy a few years ago but that apart he was always fairly even tempered; so for him to have reacted so quickly and with such intensity showed the strength of his feelings.

'She could have had a successful career, got married, had a family but Lizzie took those opportunities away from her. Manslaughter or not, no-one should allow themselves to be provoked to the point of killing another person – life is sacred. However, even if we accept that she didn't mean to do it, it was not premeditated, it still doesn't excuse what she did afterwards – throwing that poor girl's body off Hell's Drop.' Jim's voice was quivering and he was blinking rapidly.

'Jim she didn't throw her off, she would have needed superhuman strength for that. No, I believe she wasn't thinking clearly, she just took Antonia's body to a remote spot and then ...'

'Alex, there can be no justification for her actions whatever she did exactly, the result was the body of a human being lay in a remote, cold, stony gully for years, exposed to all weathers. I know she has been an amazing mother to you and I accept you love her unequivocally but what she did was unbelievable and more to the point, unforgivable.'

'You've just said it yourself, she's my mother and I love her unequivocally no matter what she has done or why. She's your wife Jim – surely she should be able to expect the same unconditional commitment from you?'

Jim lapsed into a silence that spoke volumes. He put his hands in his pockets as he had started to shake.

'She would do anything for either of us; you know that don't you?' Alex said in sad resignation.

Still Jim said nothing; he just looked at the floor.

That was undoubtedly the moment that Alex accepted something that he had probably known subconsciously for a long time – nothing could ever be the same between his mother and Jim. He had hoped they would work it out when she was released but now he realised that was not to be.

Alex had got up and walked into the bar.

When he came back to the office he found Jim standing staring into space. He looked a bit calmer. Alex passed him an orange juice.

'Where will you go Jim?' he asked.

'Thank you,' said Jim as he took the glass. 'I will stay with Sheila and Steve for a few days and then make my way to London I think. I have some old contacts down there.'

Alex knew Jim's ex-wife lived in north-west London but shrugged off the thought as it was unfair to Jim to make a connection that probably wasn't there.

Early that morning Jim had packed up his belongings and driven off, giving Alex a hug and saying he promised he would stay in touch.

Maggie said it was a shame that he had left. However when Alex had delivered some lemons to Maggie in the bar that lunchtime, he had overheard a conversation which seemed to suggest that a lot of the locals thought Jim was letting his mother down big time. So it was probably better Jim left now than stayed around making everyone's life difficult when his mother came home.

Alex now had the task of telling his mother that Jim had gone. That was not going to be easy. He hoped she would show the resilience she had demonstrated when his father had died. She was a strong lady and she had so many people rooting for her in Blenthorne. He needed to emphasise that and it might soften the blow – somehow he doubted it.

He drained the remainder of his tea, put his mug in the sink and got up to begin making some pasta to be included in that evening's menu.

Chapter 14

Reflections – 2009

Lizzie had just finished putting away some books in the geography section. She liked everything to be tidy and ready for the next day. One final check round and she turned out the lights. She loved working in the library and over the last few years had helped significantly with implementing the new layout. She also enjoyed helping inmates who were not computer literate. She had attended classes herself during her time in prison and was now proficient in both word processing and accounting software. She helped with the compilation of CVs and writing formal letters for prisoners who were keen to try to find work upon release. Also in her spare time, she had become fascinated by various ancestry websites and found the process of discovering facts about her forebears immensely rewarding.

Category D prisons housed offenders who were not considered a danger to the public. They were afforded a degree of trust and responsibility and Lizzie was soon allowed to work in the community; a privilege she had earned quickly with her willingness to throw herself into every task she was given. She visited a local day centre for the elderly twice a week and helped with meals and games. She had built up a good rapport with the senior citizens who attended and became an invaluable member of the support team.

The prison amateur dramatic club had taken on a new momentum once Lizzie arrived to breathe fresh life into it. She was able to draw on her experiences with Blenthorne Brigade and amused her fellow inmates and wardens alike with her tales of catastrophe that became a trade mark of their performances. She was also heavily involved in the craft days which saw the prison being thrown open to visitors from the community as well as friends and relatives of the inmates.

People could buy items to give as presents and all proceeds went to local causes. They also made many of the props they used in their productions.

'Bye Lizzie,' called Mandy.

'Bye Mandy – see you tomorrow,' replied Lizzie cheerfully.

'Not tomorrow, having a day off with the family. Mother-in-law's birthday, can't wait! No doubt she will find fault with everything I serve up and will locate every piece of dust that has escaped my vacuum cleaner!'

'Oh dear sounds grim – but make the best of it anyway!' called Lizzie.

Lizzie walked back to her room with a quiet smile on her face, thinking how nice Mandy Simpson was. How lovely to be part of a family who would be spending the day together; although she did have sympathy for Mandy having to entertain her in-laws.

Tomorrow would be visiting day again; it seemed to come round so quickly. Not many weeks elapsed when someone from the village did not visit. It was a bit of a journey from Blenthorne to the Yorkshire town where Lizzie was incarcerated but her boys visited regularly: Alex, Bert, Robin and Mark seemed to have sorted out a rota. Even Jono had been a couple of times.

Faye came less often but she was always pleasant when she did visit. Lizzie was hoping she would be allowed to attend Alex and Faye's wedding; she had put in an application with the governor. She was permitted some home leave for completing a portion of her sentence and complying with the regime without causing any trouble. Lizzie would never do that.

Maggie and Ruby came and shared the local gossip whenever they could and Carl accompanied them sometimes. Ruby spent most of her visits complaining about being frisked before she was allowed in, much to everyone's amusement.

Lizzie appreciated that the people she cared about did not judge her and still wanted her in their lives.

She had even had a visit from Gary Carmichael, whom she had so foolishly stabbed. She sincerely regretted that; it was a senseless spur of the moment action, much like the Antonia Mason incident if she was honest but at least he had survived the experience.

She hoped that he did not hate her – he said he didn't and he had told everyone that it had been an accident. Only she and he knew it wasn't, so that was a sort of bond between them; yes she liked Gary a lot. She had sent him a visiting order form after she had been in prison a few months but didn't really expect him to accept it; she was delighted when he did.

She reached her room and put on the light, leaving the door ajar in case anyone should want to talk to her; she then walked over to close the curtains and sat down on the bed idly picking up the novel she had been reading for the past few days.

She knew she was to receive a visitor tomorrow as she had been told to be ready to go to the reception room for 2 o'clock. She wondered if it might be Jim – she doubted it as he never came now. She kept completing visiting order forms for him but the only times he had come he hadn't been able to look her in the face. The conversation between them had been perfunctory and uncomfortable. He clearly could not understand what she had done or why. He had no ability to empathise with the situation she had found herself in. After all she had done for him. Lizzie shook her head sadly.

The prosecuting counsel and judge had accepted her manslaughter plea, so why not Jim? It was strange how people showed their true colours in adversity she thought despondently.

*

Mandy Simpson enjoyed working at the prison more than she had expected, particularly with people such as Lizzie to look after; theirs was a mutual liking and respect. Lizzie helped out with new inmates; she took anyone who was scared or lonely under her wing and certainly wasn't frightened to stand up for those who were unable to take care of themselves with some of the more forceful inmates.

Everyone respected Lizzie, from the hardnosed professional criminals who drifted in and out of prison as a way of life to first time offenders who were vulnerable and afraid. Lizzie organised them all, she wrote letters for them, she jollied them along when needed and never turned away anyone who needed her shoulder to cry on. She certainly had personality in spades!

Mandy was sure it was only a matter of time until the parole board convened to discuss her future. She would leave a huge gap in all their lives when she went home as she had become part of the composition of the place it seemed. Mandy could see no reason why Lizzie should not be released on licence, as she was so far along the road of successful rehabilitation. She should not spend a lifetime paying for a few moments' madness.

She had heard on the grapevine recently that Lizzie was thinking of providing some sort of half-way house for ex-cons once she was released with the possibility of training at her restaurant or pub and she also had a stake in the local hotel, so that would give even more possibilities. The authorities apparently liked the idea in principle. Mandy was sure if anyone could make a success of such a project it would be Lizzie. She had heard there was a house in her home village which Lizzie was thinking of buying that would be perfect accommodation for several women at a time. Although she understood it would take a little while as the property needed renovating.

She had been told when she started her job that Lizzie had admitted to the manslaughter of someone and apparently she had tried to kill a police officer but she had not been charged with that offence. Mandy did not know the circumstances but it appeared he ended up with a punctured lung but it had all been hushed up for some reason.

She was interested in the case and read up as much as she could. Lizzie had pleaded guilty to the charge and had not been brought to trial by jury; typical of the woman that her whole village wanted to speak up for her with unsolicited character testimonials. It seemed that she had been particularly kind to an elderly spinster and looked after her until she died – what a wonderful thing to do and Mandy could well believe that of Lizzie.

From the records, it appeared all the prosecution had to go on was the testimony of a small time criminal, which by itself probably would not have stood up in court. He had maintained that Lizzie had dumped a car belonging to the dead woman in Carlisle.

Popular opinion suggested that Lizzie was in fact covering up for her husband to whom she was apparently devoted. Shame he did not feel the same way Mandy thought. He never visited, well maybe once or twice a while ago but he never came near now; it seemed strange that he appeared immune to Lizzie's magnetism when the rest of the world was captivated by her.

Lockwood's restaurant was hugely successful with a reputation spread far and wide and she had heard that they had now had a favourable write up by an internationally renowned food critic. A friend had eaten there recently and told her that gossip suggested Jim Lockwood wasn't as involved as he used to be with the businesses in Blenthorne and the day-to-day running was now in the hands of his stepson.

Great, thought Mandy, she absentmindedly wondered if Ben her husband would stick around if she were to do time. She certainly hoped so! Anyway he had promised he would treat her to a meal at Lockwood's for their wedding anniversary, if he had saved up sufficiently by then to afford it.

She got into her car, turned on the ignition and headed for home.

*

Lizzie walked slowly back to her room after visiting time had finished the following afternoon. Alex had come to see her; it was lovely to see that familiar face smiling up at her as he sat at the table waiting for her to be admitted to the visitors' room. They had chatted about the businesses, the pub in particular and he had told her everyone sent their love. She asked after Jim and normally Alex just made some bland comment about him being fine and working too hard as usual but not today. No, this afternoon would stick in her mind for a long time.

'Is Jim okay darling?' she had asked Alex who was looking rather uncomfortable.

'Actually Mum that is really what I want to talk to you about today. You see Jim has made a big decision – he um, well, there is no easy way of putting it, he has decided to leave Blenthorne. He has been spending more and more time away as it is – I think he goes over to his sister's house now and again.'

'When you say leave, you mean just temporarily, until I am released?' Lizzie said quietly, intuitively knowing the answer before Alex answered.

'No, he is leaving for good I'm afraid Mum; he is in a bad way I think. He still wants to keep a stake in the restaurant but has decided not to be actively involved in the pub anymore. I think ... well that is, Carl and I believe the best thing would be to make Maggie acting manager for now. We can give her some help but she has been keeping everything together for ages anyway, so I'm sure she will be fine. Obviously I'm officially the landlord and of course Maggie has completed her personal licence training, so there are no worries there. Once you are home for good, then we can all get back to normal.' He paused and then continued:

'Carl and I have lots of ideas to run past you and I think Jono wants to expand the adventure holidays even further and is looking at hang-gliding of all things,' Alex continued in as upbeat a manner as he could muster.

'Back to normal – I don't think that things will ever be normal again my love,' said Lizzie who was then quiet for a while, seemingly pondering what she had just been told.

'The problem is ... well you see, I'm confused,' she said finally, her head swimming and her body smarting with this terrible, yet if she was honest maybe not completely unexpected news. 'You said Jim spends some time with Sheila and Steve, where does he spend the rest of it if he is away a lot?'

'He is vague about where he has been, in fact he doesn't say too much at all – I know he has been seeing a counsellor again and he seems pretty low most of the time. It doesn't help that people seem to blame him for you not being around. I know that sounds daft, but I overhear conversations nearly every day about the Blenny not being the Blenny without you behind the bar.'

'Alex, be honest with me, Maggie finally told me last week that she thinks people believe Jim had something to do with Antonia's death. Do you get that impression?'

'Well ... if you are putting me on the spot then yes. But it is not just that, I think it is more that everyone genuinely misses you and wants you back.'

'Everyone apart from Jim, is that what you are saying? He never visits me. I can't believe he could turn his back on me – I would forgive him anything you know. I had thought maybe it was this place, the prison that he could not cope with but maybe it is actually me that he can't bear any more. There is something else isn't there Alex?' asked Lizzie intuitively.

'Mum, I think you ought to know, there is a suggestion that he has been going down south; to London.'

'London, why's he going to London? Oh yes of course! Sarah lives there doesn't she? I heard recently that she and Ashley Duncan had separated,' sighed Lizzie in sad resignation. 'Jim will be spending his time with her.'

'Well I don't know about that – there could be any number of reasons – he could still have friends there I suppose – he did come from that area originally didn't he – I mean London is a big place he might not be seeing anyone in particular.'

Alex's voice seemed to trail away and Lizzie didn't really listen as closely as she should when he changed the subject to talk about the details of the wedding arrangements which were now gathering pace.

As she waved Alex goodbye, she thought how cruel life was and how ironic.

She walked along the corridor in a daze. She encountered a couple of fellow inmates on her way to her room and had the briefest of chats with them, extricating herself as quickly as possible. She got to her room and shut the door behind her – she normally left it ajar; "open house at Lizzie's" was the popular mantra. However on this occasion she needed some time and space to think.

She sat on her bed and pulled the duvet around her shoulders as she felt suddenly chilled. She clutched her arms around her knees, hugging herself and gently began to rock backwards and forwards. She had had doubts about Jim for some time; the conversation today with Alex proved she was right. In fact after her guilty plea, it was her son not her husband whom she had nominated as licensee of the Blenny. She told herself that it was to spare him the responsibility but maybe she had always subconsciously known that Jim was flaky.

So he was going to abandon her. As she had told Alex, she would have forgiven Jim anything; absolutely anything. Well that was clearly a one way street!

After about half an hour of crying quietly, she shook herself out of her self-pitying stupor. This won't beat me, she resolved, I have been through worse – some of the shadows from the past tried to push their way through to the front of her mind. She thrust them aside and thought of positive things.

She had to stop allowing her heart to rule her head, she needed to think clearly and concentrate on planning her future.

Her continuing friendship with Gary would do her no harm in the eyes of the parole board; she would play that up to the hilt.

The fact that the police didn't really believe her story completely had played in her favour too; they implied she was shielding someone. However they had no evidence against Jim so whatever they thought and suggested privately, the fact remained that Lizzie Lockwood was serving a sentence for crimes she admitted to and insisted she had committed alone.

In light of Jim's behaviour, it might be beneficial to perhaps not attempt to dissuade people from thinking she had selflessly taken responsibility for the actions of someone she loved.

They had not asked her about Naomi so she had not told them – innocence by omission as she liked to think of it. She had been a good friend to Naomi for years. In fact if Naomi had not become such a liability, she would not have needed to act as she had. She really had no choice in the matter; Naomi had become collateral damage. Everyone had paid tribute to the way in which she cared for her. Certainly she had made Naomi's life much more pleasant than it otherwise might have been towards the end.

She thought again about Gary and his loyalty towards her, without a doubt her sentence would have been far longer if she had gone down for stabbing him. Yes, loyalty was not too strong a word for it. He was one in a million. Then her thoughts turned again to Jim.

Her heart sank to even lower depths as she again realised he had left her – not a lot of loyalty there!

He would no doubt meet up with Sarah again, if he had not done so already – even if Sheila did not put them in touch, with social media sites now so prevalent it was not difficult to find people from the past. Once in contact, they could chat every day on line or by mobile. So even if his current trips to London were not to see her, they soon would be! She had seen the body language between them on the day of Sheila's birthday party a few years ago. She felt sick as she thought about it.

He could at least have had the decency to come and tell her to her face, but no, he was just going to slink off and abandon her. She had clearly misjudged him totally. She really just had to accept that she cared too much about people who were unworthy of her trust and love.

Look at Richard. Another total miscalculation on her part; she had given him a second chance and just look at how he had repaid her.

He had promised faithfully that he would have no further contact with Alison, the home-wrecking witch from Woking with whom he had had an affair prior to their move to

Blenthorne. So what had happened? Within a year of their "fresh start" she had followed him north and set up home in Carlisle.

How stupid did he think Lizzie was? All those "business meetings" and "development opportunities" he was chasing. All the time he was with the witch.

Did he think she did not notice that when he arrived home he was freshly showered – even in the middle of the afternoon! He could at least have pretended he had been playing squash, that would account for the smell of shampoo, the newly applied deodorant and aftershave.

Did he think she did not notice when money disappeared from their account – never a lot but she was sharp enough to spot it. Stupid man; writing cheques to flower shops but never thinking she might realise that the flowers themselves were never delivered. Then there was the jewellery of course; on the last occasion a diamond necklace if she was not mistaken. No need to speculate whose neck that adorned! How many blinking salads and sandwiches had she had to prepare to pay for that she wondered paradoxically!

She got up and started to pace around the room. Oh yes – she knew exactly when the affair started up again. She had heard his side of the late night telephone conversations when he crept downstairs thinking she was asleep; did he not realise that as a mother, she never sleep soundly just in case her child was ill and needed her?

'Yes, I will when the time is right; you know that's what I want more than anything but I can't get away at the moment. No of course I won't, we will sell it I promise, just as soon as I can get things in order ... Well because it will fetch a better price with planning permission in place for the restaurant ... No, she won't have a choice; she can't stay here without my share of the business. Yes soon ... Sweetheart, you have my word.'

Of course he could have gone to the phone box across the road to make his clandestine calls but no he did it from home, he clearly thought she was deaf as well as daft. Did he really think she never checked the phone bill – all those calls to the same number?

His duplicity knew no bounds. Even now that made her blood boil; she had given up her whole life for him. She had uprooted herself and Alex and moved to Blenthorne at his behest, it was all his idea and for what? He was going to leave her anyway, maybe not immediately but soon enough. He had already casually dropped into the conversation that they would make a good profit when they sold up – not if, but when they sold up!

From what he had told the witch, she knew he would want half of everything; she could not raise enough capital to buy him out and they would have to sell the pub. Her lovely life in the Lakes would be at an end, unless she got a live-in manager's job at another pub – possibly a national chain – but it would not be the Blenny, it would not be her home – she would be an employee not the landlady – she had status in Blenthorne, she had friends. It was unthinkable and she could not let it happen. There had to be a way out of it.

He had been the one who had wanted to move to Blenthorne but she had been the one that fitted into the place and with the people. His plan had been to combine the two bars, thereby denying her regulars of their local. So what if they didn't spend much money. The Blenny was part of their community. No, something had had to be done, there had been no alternative.

Poor Richard – life was so cruel. She really had loved him and all she asked of him was fidelity, she had forgiven his behaviour once and this was how he had repaid her.

She had sobbed and sobbed when she realised he had been killed in the accident.

She did not want him to die. If he had just crashed the car and been incapacitated for a while then he could not keep sneaking off to Carlisle and Lizzie would make sure he could have no access to a phone. That way when the witch did not see him, did not hear from him and could not visit him, she would leave. There would be nothing for her here – she would just get back on her broomstick and fly out of their lives for good.

Lizzie had suggested he go to The Swan at Hangmere on the night he died to check out their evening menu. The forecast was terrible. He always drove too fast, she had spent her life clinging to the seat or the door and pressing her foot down on the non-existent brake on the passenger side, so it was a fair bet he would try to hammer home along the Overton Pass in poor road conditions.

She had told the police he had been a good driver, but the reality was if she was not in the car to keep him in check, he would behave like a reckless racing driver. That was clearly what happened on that fateful night.

As it was, events spiralled out of control; that was the problem with uncontrolled variables – you could not be sure of the exact outcome. Being mindful of this, she made sure she never allowed Alex to travel in the car with Richard after she had tampered with his brakes. It had not been a difficult job for the daughter of a mechanic.

Silly foolish Richard – she had loved him but he proved to be unworthy of her. She thought of him for a while and a veil of despondency descended upon her.

As was usual when she got into that frame of mind, Caroline also appeared.

Dear cute little Caroline, her deceased school friend. She had loved Caroline like a sister and so very much enjoyed the holidays they spent together at Caroline's uncle's holiday cottage by the sea in Cornwall. Every year Caroline's parents invited her to stay with them as Caroline was an only child like Lizzie.

The day before Caroline's accident, she had boasted to Lizzie that she had a new best friend, a girl called Wendy who had just moved in next door to her and they would be sitting together from September. Wendy didn't know anyone so the headmistress had spoken to Caroline's parents to ask if Caroline would be her guide and companion until she found her feet.

Apparently Wendy had all the latest toys – not only a teenage fashion doll with loads of clothes and high heels but also accessories such as a bedroom, a boat and a boyfriend! Lizzie hadn't been allowed things like that as her mother said with a loud sniff that they were "inappropriate". Lizzie couldn't imagine why.

Wendy also had a magnetic word game which she had lent to Caroline so that she could take it on holiday. Lizzie refused to play with it.

What could she offer as a friendship enhancer? A silly baby doll dressed all in pink that cried when you filled its mouth with water and squeezed its tummy. The first time Lizzie tried it she got the water everywhere much to her mother's deep displeasure – not only that, but the doll's eyelashes fell out.

Worse still, her parents bought her a dolls' pram – like she was ever going to play with that! Blinking contraption stood in the corner of her bedroom collecting dust for years. Her mother had called her a "nasty ungrateful and undeserving little girl" and said she would give it to someone else who would appreciate such a lovely present. She very much hoped her mother would keep her promise but sadly much to Lizzie's disappointment, she never did. So there it stayed buried under whatever detritus Lizzie could pile on top of it to hide the horrid thing. She usually gave it a kick on the way past for good measure.

Caroline dropped her bombshell on the second day of their holiday.

'I doubt you will be coming here again Lizzie,' she had said spitefully as she swung on the gatepost leading to the cottage. 'I will probably ask Wendy next year.'

Lizzie made up her mind immediately what had to be done. That was the first time that betrayal had reared its head in her life she noted with a wry smile.

You won't be asking Wendy she thought and how right she had been.

The following day just after dawn, Lizzie had woken Caroline and suggested they go for an early morning dip without telling anyone. They left the cottage quietly, having slipped their swimming costumes on under their clothes and tucked their towels under their arms. Lizzie had chosen to take her bath towel rather than her swimming towel but Caroline didn't seem to notice. They made their way to the jetty where Caroline's uncle moored his boat.

They stripped off their outer clothes and Lizzie slipped on her swimming hat; a ghastly pink affair with flowers all over it. Her mother insisted she wear it for lessons and everyone laughed at her. Today though, she wanted to keep her hair dry.

Caroline had wanted to go to the shoreline and just paddle. What a wimp she was. Lizzie insisted they go to the jetty so that they could dangle their feet over the side. After a while Lizzie suggested they dive in. She was a strong swimmer but Caroline was less confident.

'You go first,' said Lizzie as Caroline stood up tentatively. 'Not scared are you?'

'No, of course I'm not,' replied Caroline hesitantly.

'Good – in you go then,' said Lizzie as she gave her an almighty shove.

She could still remember Caroline splashing around with her head bobbing up and down as she spluttered and coughed and tried to get her breath.

'Lizzie help me please, I'm going to drown. I can't reach the ground with my feet,' she squealed, gulping as she tried to keep her head above water.

'Of course you can't, if it's deep enough for a boat, it must be too deep for you to put your feet on the bottom, unless you were about ten feet tall of course!' said Lizzie lightly as she danced along the jetty, practising her ballet steps, seemingly unaware of the danger facing Caroline.

After a few moments she looked down and was disappointed to see that Caroline had made it to one of the wooden supports and had her head and shoulders out of the water; she was still breathing loudly as she filled her lungs with huge inhalations of air but had stopped coughing. Lizzie had hoped to frighten her a bit more than that, so she jumped in.

'Hang on Carrie; I'll be with you in a moment,' she said as she swam the short distance to her friend.

Once there, she persuaded Caroline to let go of the wooden support and said she would help her get out. As soon as Caroline was free of anything to grab hold of Lizzie pushed herself up in the water and pressed her hand down on Caroline's head, completely submerging it. Caroline's limbs were flailing about and Lizzie had to keep her at arm's length to stop from getting hit.

With the logic of a nine year old, she really just intended to hold Caroline down briefly and then let her bob up again to give her the chance to promise not to abandon her in favour of Wendy and she would have to swear not to tell anyone what had happened that morning.

However she left it a bit too long; she suddenly realised the flailing arms were still floating limply in the water. When she let go, Caroline did not bob up to the surface spluttering and coughing, she just remained face down and lifeless.

That was not what she wanted at all.

Thinking quickly, Lizzie thrust Caroline under the boat and got out of the water as fast as she could. She dried herself briefly on her bath towel and leaving Caroline's towel and clothes in a pile; put on her own things and made her way back to the cottage. It was still only just after 6 o'clock in the morning. She put her towel back in the bathroom on the radiator and stashed her costume inside her swimming hat and put these into her case. She then got into bed and appeared to be sound asleep when Caroline's mum came in to wake them a little after 8:30 a.m.

'Good morning girls! Oh Lizzie, where's Caroline?' she asked looking at the empty bed.

'Goodness me, I don't know,' said Lizzie, wide eyed and innocent as she emerged from the covers, yawning.

After checking she was not in the cottage, Lizzie along with Caroline's parents and uncle make a search of the garden. While they were all outside and preoccupied, Lizzie slipped back into the cottage to dry off her swimming costume with the hairdryer in case anyone checked later and found it to be damp. Once it was dry, she put the costume and the ghastly hat into a drawer.

On returning outside, Lizzie then remembered that Caroline had said last evening that she wanted them to go swimming early that morning, but Lizzie was not keen to go unaccompanied and told her it was a bad idea. Maybe Caroline had gone anyway, so perhaps they should check the beach.

They all rushed down to the beach calling Caroline's name. Caroline's mother said they should call the police to report her missing but her father and uncle said that was too soon for that and she would be bound to turn up.

And turn up she did.

By lunchtime when the police and coastguard had been called, her body was found floating a little downstream from where the boat was moored.

Lizzie was distraught as anyone would be who had lost their best friend. The gentle questions of the WPC had established that Lizzie had not woken when Caroline had left the room and could throw no light on the circumstances surrounding her death.

The coroner recorded a verdict of accidental death by drowning. Lizzie was heartbroken. If only Caroline and been a loyal friend, it need not have happened. As it was, Caroline, silly, spiteful, sugary-sweet Caroline didn't get the opportunity to snub Lizzie and take Wendy to Cornwall the following year.

In fact Caroline never went to Cornwall again.

At the beginning of the new term at school the headmistress had stood up in assembly and told the pupils of the terrible accident that had befallen Lizzie's best friend Caroline. It was subsequently agreed that Lizzie needed special support and gentle handling from everyone. She embraced the sympathy of her classmates and teachers and struggled on through her pain.

To take her mind off the tragedy, it was suggested Lizzie should look after Wendy as a way to distract her from dwelling on the events of the summer holidays.

Somehow the magnetic word game had been found with the base broken into pieces in the garden of the Cornwall cottage. However it was alright because Wendy's mother bought her a new one and also one for Lizzie, as she felt so sorry for her.

Lizzie liked Wendy and was particularly pleased when Wendy invited her to tea and introduced her to her fashion doll, complete with accessories and boyfriend. She also introduced Lizzie to her older brother. She remained friends with Wendy Tennyson right through school. Afterwards she went to college and Wendy went to work in Spain and decided to stay.

Then of course she had met up with Wendy's brother again …

Lizzie snapped herself out of her melancholy memories and shivered a little as she tidied her hair and left her cell to go to the dining room for tea.

*

A few weeks later Lizzie woke up in a cold sweat. The shadows were surrounding her again. Richard and Caroline had both been in her dream; they were pointing at her. Over the years she had thought about them intermittently but now they seemed to crowd in on her every thought.

A few nights ago they had been joined by Antonia and Naomi; really that was almost too much to bear. She turned over in bed and told herself not to be so silly.

She clearly had too much time on her hands so she threw herself into the planning of the next am-dram production – she had suggested they do a comedy and that seemed a popular choice; but they were limited in their selection as all the parts had to be played by women.

She realised she needed to keep her mind occupied so that she did not have time for dark thoughts. She needed to be planning for the future and looking to her release. This would happen she had been reliably informed in no more than a few months. She had things to think about; or one thing in particular – Jim.

Did he really think he could just leave her? She needed to decide what to do about him. He had let her down very badly. There was no rush, the wedding before then and some home visits to acclimatise prior to release.

Then she could turn her attention to the problem of her errant husband.

She had learned a valuable lesson from the incidents with Antonia and Gary; the imprudence of thinking one can get away with knee jerk reactions. Things needed to be unrushed and thought through properly so as to get them right. Look at the way she had orchestrated Naomi's demise. No one ever suspected it was anything other than natural causes. Her planning had been meticulous and that was what was needed now.

She settled down into bed again, having had a drink of water. She was calmer now.

It was a long time since she had visited London. She would go there again after she was released. Lots of people lived in London of course – she wondered if she might bump into anyone she knew ...

*

Shortly afterwards Lizzie received a handwritten letter from Jim in his usual scrawl:

Lizzie, please forgive me,

I'm sorry I shouldn't have left it so long before getting in touch; I have tried several times to write but somehow I couldn't find the right words.

I know that I should have come to tell you this in person and I have no real excuse other than that I find it too difficult to see you and talk to you face to face. I keep wondering how things might have been if you had never encountered Antonia Mason. We were building a good life together and I had everything I could have wanted with you and Alex.

Sadly, the reality of the situation is that I cannot reconcile myself with what happened on that terrible day and as much as I have tried, I cannot understand or accept the decisions you made and the actions you took and don't think I ever will. For that reason I have made a momentous decision – I believe my future lies away from Blenthorne.

I know that you are to have some acclimatisation days soon, prior to your release and I think it is better that I leave before you come home. I know you will receive a warm welcome as everyone has missed you immensely.

I plan to leave my investment in the restaurant for the time being if that is okay with you and Alex. I have contacted Robin and Mark regarding the hotel.

I will always be grateful to you for the chance you gave me when I applied for the bar job. You were instrumental in getting me back on my feet and I can never repay the debt I owe you.

I sincerely wish you a happy future and hope that you can remember me as someone who shared your life for a while and with whom you had some good times.

Take care Lizzie,

Jim

Lizzie re-read the letter. "I" at the start of almost every paragraph she noted and then all through the letter "I", "I", "I". Yes, all about him, never a thought about what she had been through and what she had done for him, however misguided she had been.

Lizzie tore a small strip off the top of the letter and put it in her pocket. The rest she screwed into a ball and lobbed into the bin.

She swallowed deeply and wiped her eyes. There was a morning craft session that she needed to get to and she was already running late.

'Lizzie where are you?' called Lucy Harris, a shy girl who had only just arrived and never liked to enter a room alone. 'Can we go to the card-making class together?'

'Of course we can Lovely Lucy, I'm coming,' called Lizzie brightly. She left her room and closed the door.

Chapter 15

Epilogue – 2010

Detective Inspector Gary Carmichael was getting ready to leave his office for the night. Just before he turned off his computer he noticed the time - 10:45 p.m. He realised he hadn't stopped for dinner. The canteen would be shut now. A bit late to go to the pub he thought with a sigh. Never mind he would have some toast when he finally made it back to his flat, or cereal if the bread had run out. No milk though, he realised with an air of resignation, he would need to get some from the petrol station en route.

He then indulged in what he liked to think of as a displacement activity, which was basically anything that would put off going home, so he had a quick flick through the day's news. He had looked at lunchtime and expected the headlines to be much the same unless something startling had happened that afternoon.

He had read that the ash cloud from the volcanic eruption in Iceland was still hanging over the country and thousands of holiday makers were stranded abroad as planes across Europe were grounded. That might affect a couple of his colleagues who were due back in a day or so. The general election campaign was gathering pace he noted with disinterest and was about to close the tab when something caught his eye.

"Body Found at Government Advisor's Home
Police were today called to the former home of Sir Ashley Duncan, where the body of a white male was discovered. Lady Duncan, the ex-wife of the millionaire property developer is believed to now own the property.
Detective Inspector Peter Hughes said the man was believed to be in his 40s and is thought to be Lady Duncan's first husband James Lockwood, who neighbours confirmed,

lived with her at the property. The exact cause of death would be established shortly but initial sources suggest that it appeared to be a suicide or accidental death and a note was found at the scene.

Lady Duncan was believed to have been attending a charitable function in the city at the time of the incident and raised the alarm upon her return."

The article went on to list Ashley Duncan's achievements both in the field of politics as well as commerce and industry. It also briefly noted that Sarah had married Ashley after the breakdown of her first marriage and they subsequently divorced last year. Gary gave up and clicked the page closed. He turned off the computer and picking up his jacket from the back of his chair, left for home.

He thought about Lizzie Lockwood on his journey. What on earth was life going to throw at her next? He had heard that she had been released on licence a couple of months ago and had returned home to Blenthorne. He was leaving it a respectable time before he got in touch – just to make sure she was okay – no other reason.

He had visited her once in prison at her request. She had looked thin and gaunt as she entered the room. She pulled out the chair opposite his at the small table where he was sitting. She had sat down and gazed at him. He saw such genuine sorrow and regret when they had met face to face.

She sat quietly with her hands in her lap in the visiting room and she leaned forward to emphasise what she was saying.

She apologised sincerely for the injury she had inflicted upon him that fateful day when she was arrested. She said she could not begin to thank him for the statement he had made which meant she did not have to serve time for that offence.

He would have needed a heart made of steel for it not to melt as he looked into those big dark eyes, filled with tears.

Her chin quivered as she tried to maintain her composure. She had brushed her tears away with her hand and pushed her hair behind her ears as she regained a bit of her spirit. The old

Lizzie shone out for a moment as she told him she understood he could never forgive her and indeed she could never forgive herself for her action, but she cared about him deeply and wished him well for the future.

'Please don't hate me,' she had said simply.

He had swallowed and softly replied that he couldn't hate her even if he tried.

She had got up and left the visiting room without looking back.

She had sent him a card every Christmas just signed "Lizzie" and he had sent one back each year with a brief message to say he hoped she was okay. He continued to think of her as he drove along the familiar roads towards his flat.

He reached home, having completely forgotten to stop at the petrol station for milk and let himself into the quiet still flat with his door key. He picked up the post and turned on the hall light. He dropped his key fob into a small pottery bowl on the hallway table and taking off his jacket, draped it over the top.

He entered the kitchen and went to the fridge. The uninspiring contents didn't give him much to choose from but he selected a lager and found half a bag of peanuts in the cupboard above the washing machine. He put the light on in the lounge area and fished his mobile phone out of the right hand pocket of his trousers and turned it off. He then dropped it gently onto the coffee table in front of him. He flopped down on the sofa, opened the lager and thrust a handful of the nuts into his mouth. He loosened his tie as he pushed the cushions away to make himself more comfortable.

He absentmindedly looked for the remote which he finally located down the side of the sofa, with what seemed to be a boiled sweet attached; he picked it off tentatively with thumb and forefinger and threw it in the direction of the overfull bin – it missed and landed on the floor. He got up and wiped his sticky hand on a tea towel he found lying on the dining table.

He turned the television on; it was permanently tuned to one of the sports channels. He had no idea what he was watching as once his train of thought had turned to Lizzie, there was little he could do to stop himself going over the whole sorry string of events again, as he had so many times before, as it just did not feel right.

He had been a detective for a long time and a crime was like a jigsaw puzzle in many ways. When you had the pieces in the correct place they fitted exactly and you knew it. However in this case, the pieces almost fitted but not quite.

He was still not convinced and never would be that the whole truth had come out. As soon as he mentioned to Lizzie that Jim was helping with enquiries into the death of Antonia Mason, her manner changed totally. She had turned on him and embedded those blasted scissors into his chest. That was a complete aberration on her part; totally out of character. However such were her feelings for Jim that she lashed out in desperation at the thought he might be in trouble.

He marvelled at the intensity of her commitment to her husband and the lengths she would go to in order to safeguard him. He couldn't imagine Cheryl ever doing that for him, even when they were together.

He would bet a pound to a penny that Jim Lockwood knew more about the death of Antonia Mason than he was prepared to admit. He just sat back and let his wife carry the can. Gary was sure that Luke Farmer was right; Lizzie had driven the car to Carlisle however, being an accessory after the fact does not make her guilty of manslaughter. He was convinced her confession was for one reason alone – to save Jim.

He had gone to see Jim once he had recovered sufficiently from his pneumothorax. Just before Lizzie's court hearing where her guilty plea would be submitted, he had rung Jim and arranged to meet him at Long Lawn Hotel in Rowendale. Their meeting had been quite amiable to begin with. They had met in the bar and had a drink, sitting together at a table near a window overlooking the garden. After a couple of minutes, Jim started to fidget and became ill at ease. He kept twisting and untwisting his hands and he was blinking rapidly.

Gary hoped he had been non-confrontational but he had made it clear to Jim that if he knew anything more than he had already put in his witness statement, now was the time to get it off his chest. Did he really want his wife, the woman who had helped him turn his life around, to go to prison for manslaughter?

Of course Jim was camping on the day in question with Alex as well as several other boys and helpers. However, it was impossible to know the exact date when Antonia was killed. Jim could have stashed the car in the barn for days or weeks without anyone being any the wiser and then asked Lizzie to drive it to Carlisle while he was away.

Jim was pretty convincing, Gary would concede that. If he was a juror and Jim stood up in court and said he was not guilty of anything, Gary was sure he would believe him. Gary knew Lizzie and believed she would do anything for Jim – even cover up a serious crime for him. Jim had left abruptly after about five minutes and he never saw him again.

Gary was as certain as he could be that Jim Lockwood was responsible for the death of Antonia Mason, so really he had two victims – Antonia and Lizzie.

He knew via the grapevine that he was not alone in that belief. Many people in Blenthorne also thought that Lizzie had pleaded guilty to keep Jim out of the frame. Apparently once Lizzie went to prison Jim's time in Blenthorne was not a happy one. What a shame!

He knew that Jim had left Blenthorne before Lizzie was released and it appeared from what he had read in the paper today, he had subsequently set up home with his ex in London, how utterly insensitive.

Well maybe at last he had developed a conscience and taken his own life – cowardly way to avoid justice in Gary's opinion for what that was worth.

He drained his can of lager and, glancing at the overfull bin in the corner of the lounge, left the empty on the coffee table. He went over to the bin, picked up the sticky boiled sweet from the carpet and then balanced it carefully on the top of the other debris. He would tidy up sometime; definitely before the boys came to stay, otherwise they might report back to Cheryl that he was living like a slob; it was true but he did not need her on his case again.

He took the remaining nuts back to the kitchen and stuffed them back in a cupboard. He turned out the lights and made his way to the shower prior to going to bed.

A bit later after getting into bed, he thumped his pillow into submission and thought again about Lizzie and how she was coping. He hoped she had not seen the newspaper; however to the best of his knowledge she and Jim were still married so presumably she had been contacted as his next of kin. He found himself wondering about the note that had been found with the body. It would be interesting to know what was in it. He would follow that up in the morning when he had time.

*

The following morning after reading his emails, he rang to speak to the DI in charge of Jim's case on the basis that he had known the deceased for several years.

He introduced himself and went on to say that Jim Lockwood had been a person of interest in a manslaughter case a few years ago. He would be interested to know what the suicide note had said, in case it threw any more light on the circumstances surrounding the death of Antonia Mason.

'Ah, I remember now,' said DI Hughes. 'Wasn't there a bit of doubt at the time that the wife had actually committed the crime, the feeling was she was carrying the can for her husband but wouldn't be shaken from her story? Yes I thought the name was familiar; that has saved me doing any further digging, thanks. It looks pretty straightforward though, it appears he overdosed on prescription drugs.'

He went on, 'To answer your question; basically the note was very brief and handwritten on a scrap of paper – not even a whole sheet – mind you, he was depressed I am given to understand, so I don't suppose we will ever know what exactly was in his mind that day. I don't think it will shed any more light on the case you are thinking of – it wasn't a suicide note as such, it was a note to his wife, it just said:

"Lizzie, please forgive me, I'm sorry I shouldn't have left ..."

Then it just tailed off. So no real help I'm afraid, sorry mate.'

They chatted briefly for another couple of minutes then Gary thanked him and ended the call.

Well that was a turn up! So Jim regretted leaving Lizzie – well so he should. It was a bit drastic to actually kill himself though – why didn't he just go home, Gary was sure Lizzie would have taken him back in a heartbeat.

Maybe Jim had a sudden attack of guilt which had become overwhelming. Gary pondered the realistic possibility that no-one would ever know the full truth as Lizzie would never give Jim away, even in death.

One thing was for sure, Lizzie was definitely going to need a lot of support, particularly when she found out what Jim had written in that note; brief though it was.

He supposed he should be wary of her – she had stabbed him after all and prior to that had used him as a pawn in her plan to be free of Luke Farmer when he had tried to blackmail her. Somehow though he just couldn't stop thinking about her.

He would call her today to see if she needed any practical help – just as a friend of course. At least now he had an excuse to make contact. In fact, no time like the present.

He pulled his phone out of his pocket, pressed out the number and waited for a connection. If ever a moment in life can be defined as "life-changing" then for Gary Carmichael, this undoubtedly would prove to be it...